FANTASTIC FOUR
THE FLAMES OF BATTLE

STAN LEE ● JACK KIRBY

FANTASTIC FOUR
THE FLAMES OF BATTLE

CONTENTS

MARVEL **POCKETBOOK** Fantastic Four: The Flames Of Battle

Fantastic Four: The Flames Of Battle. Marvel Pocketbook Vol. 4. Contains material originally published in magazine form as Fantastic Four (Vol. I) #68-73 and annual 5. First printing 2007. Published by Panini Publishing, a division of Panini UK Limited. Mike Riddell, Managing Director. Alan O'Keefe, Managing Editor. Mark Irvine, Production Manager. Marco M. Lupoi, Publishing Director Europe. Ed Hammond, Reprint Editor. Tim Warran-Smith, Designer. Office of publication: Panini House, Coach and Horses Passage, The Pantiles, Tunbridge Wells, Kent TN2 5UJ. Copyright © 1967, 1968 & 2007 Marvel Characters, Inc. All rights reserved. All characters featured in this edition and the distinctive names and likenesses thereof are trademarks of Marvel Characters, Inc. No similarity between any of the names, characters, persons and/or institutions in this edition with those of any living or dead person or institution is intended, and any such similarity which may exist is purely coincidental. This publication may not be sold, except by authorised dealers, and is sold subject to the condition that it shall not be sold or distributed with any part of its cover or markings removed, nor in a mutilated condition. This publication is produced under licence from Marvel Characters, Inc. through Panini S.p.A. Printed in Italy. ISBN: 978-1-84653-045-6

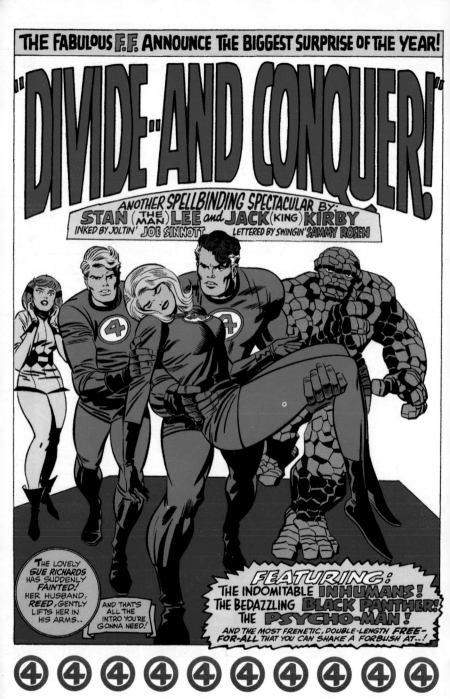

THE FABULOUS **F.F.** ANNOUNCE THE BIGGEST SURPRISE OF THE YEAR!

"DIVIDE"AND CONQUER!"

ANOTHER *SPELLBINDING* SPECTACULAR BY:
STAN (THE MAN) LEE and JACK (KING) KIRBY
INKED BY JOLTIN' JOE SINNOTT   LETTERED BY SWINGIN' SAMMY ROSEN

THE LOVELY SUE RICHARDS HAS SUDDENLY *FAINTED!* HER HUSBAND, *REED,* GENTLY LIFTS HER IN HIS ARMS...

AND THAT'S ALL THE INTRO YOU'RE GONNA NEED!

FEATURING:
THE INDOMITABLE **INHUMANS!**
THE BEDAZZLING **BLACK PANTHER!**
THE **PSYCHO-MAN!**
AND THE MOST FRENETIC, DOUBLE-LENGTH **FREE-FOR-ALL** THAT YOU CAN SHAKE A FORBUSH AT...!

[6]

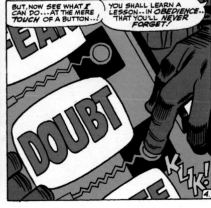

[12]

HE IS *UNCONSCIOUS!* YOU MAY TAKE *COMPONENT FIVE* NOW!

HE WAS *MAGNIFICENT!* INSTEAD OF COLLAPSING IN FEAR--HE *FOUGHT BACK*--EVEN THOUGH IT WAS *HOPELESS* FROM THE START!

FOR, THE *IMAGINARY CREATURE* HE FOUGHT WAS HIS *OWN GREAT POWER...*THE *ONE* THING HE HAS ALWAYS *FEARED* WOULD DAMAGE OTHERS IF IT EVER GOT OUT OF *CONTROL!*

WHAT ABOUT THE *GIRL?*

LEAVE HER! WE ONLY DO WHAT *PSYCHO-MAN TELLS* US TO DO, REMEMBER?

THIS IS WHAT WE CAME FOR!

THEN LET US *DEPART!*

NOW, WITH THE MATERIAL WITHIN THAT LEAD-LINED CASE, I CAN CREATE A *GIANT-SIZED PSYCHO RAY...*

A RAY CAPABLE OF AFFECT-ING THE *EMOTIONS* OF EVERY *MAN, WOMAN,* AND *CHILD* ON EARTH!

COMPONENT FIVE WAS THE *FINAL ELEMENT* I NEED BEFORE COMPLETING MY *GREATEST* PROJECT!

AND, WHOEVER CONTROLS THE *EMOTIONS* OF THE HELPLESS HUMAN RACE THEN BECOMES THE TOTAL *MASTER* OF ALL HUMANITY!

AND *WE* RULE RIGHT ALONG *WITH* YOU... RIGHT?

PERHAPS...IF IT SHOULD SO *PLEASE* ME! NOW--CARRY OUT YOUR ORDERS!

WE MUST TRANSPORT *COMPONENT FIVE* TO MY HIDDEN BASE IN THE *CARIBBEAN,* WHERE I CAN WORK ON IT *UNDISTURBED* WHILE THE THREE OF YOU MAINTAIN PERPETUAL *VIGIL!*

I HOPE WE GET A GOOD *HEAD START* BEFORE THE *THING* WAKES UP! IF HE EVER TEARS INTO US WHEN YOU'RE *NOT* THERE WITH YOUR *PSYCHO RAY...*

HAVE YOU *FORGOT-TEN?* BY THE TIME WE CAN BE *FOUND,* THE WORLD WILL BE *MINE!*

WE BELIEVE YOU! JUST MAKE SURE YOU *CONVINCE* THE *THING!*

8.

BUT NOW, INASMUCH AS THE ENTIRE *GLOBE* IS MARVEL'S MIXED-UP BATTLEGROUND, LET'S VISIT *PANTHER ISLAND,* SO NAMED FOR THE BILLIONAIRE WAKANDA CHIEFTAIN WHO HAS JUST *PURCHASED* IT...

ACCORDING TO OUR *RADAR,* IT IS *THERE* THAT THE *INTRUDERS* HAVE LANDED.

BACK TO YOUR *POSTS,* THEN! IT IS TIME FOR THE *BLACK PANTHER* TO PROWL.... *ALONE!*

IF THOSE WHO HAVE LANDED COME IN *PEACE,* THEY SHALL BE *RECEIVED* IN PEACE!

BUT *WOE* TO ANY WHO DESIRE *HARM* TO THE PEOPLE OF THE *WAKANDAS!*

AT MY *HEELS...* LIVING STRANDS OF *HAIR...*ATTEMPTING TO *TRAP* ME!

BUT, THE *BLACK PANTHER* IS NOT SO EASILY ENSNARED!!

A *FEMALE...*WITH SCARLET TRESSES THAT OBEY HER EVERY WHIM!

KARNAK! HE IS *STRONGER* THAN WE THOUGHT! HE *ATTACKS* US!

STAND BACK, MEDUSA! I SHALL DROP HIM IN HIS *TRACKS!*

NOTHING CAN RESIST MY SHATTER-ING *HAND SLAM!*

9.

THAT *EXPRESSION*--ON BLACK BOLT'S FACE!!

THE *DANGER* HE SENSES IS BOTH *IMMEDIATE*-- AND *DEADLY!*

IF ONLY *TRITON*-- AND *GORGON*-- COULD BE HERE *TOO!*

GORGON HAS GONE UPON AN ERRAND! HE WILL *RETURN* SHORTLY!

BUT, *TRITON* HAS ACCOMPANIED *CRYSTAL* TO THE CITY OF *NEW YORK*--

TO VISIT THE *HUMAN TORCH!*

THE *TORCH!!* THEN-- WE SHARE A FRIEND IN *COMMON!*

SO--I TELL YOU *THIS*--

IF DANGER THREATENS US *TOGETHER*-- WE SHARE IT *TOGETHER*--AND WE SHALL *DEFEAT* IT-- *TOGETHER!*

THEY DO NOT SUSPECT THAT *I*, TOO, AM A *KING!*

YET, NEVER HAVE I SEEN A MONARCH WITH THE *COMPLETE COMMAND*--THE TOTAL SENSE OF *POWER*--WHICH HE WHOM THEY CALL *BLACK BOLT* POSSESSES!

WHATEVER THE *DANGER* MAY *BE*, IT LIES BENEATH OUR *FEET!*

WE ALL CAN SENSE IT *NOW!*

BE *SILENT*--ALL-- AS I MENTALLY *PROBE* FOR WHAT WE SEEK!

THE NATURAL POWER OF MY *BRAIN* WILL GUIDE MY PEERLESS *FINGERS* TO THE *WEAKEST POINT* AMONGST THE ROCKS BELOW!

YOU *DID* IT! YOU SHATTERED THE REEF'S SURFACE LIKE AN *EGGSHELL!*

BUT, WHAT IS THIS *DOME* THAT WAS HIDDEN BELOW??

BEFORE MEDUSA'S STARTLED QUESTION CAN BE ANSWERED, A SUDDEN *SHOCK WAVE* LASHES OUT, WITH THE FURY OF A THUNDERCLAP--!!

KARNAK!!

12

[17]

BUT, BACK IN NEW YORK, THERE IS *ANOTHER* SURPRISE AWAITING US--OF A SLIGHTLY *DIFFERENT* SORT--

HEY, STRETCHO--WHAT'RE YA *WAITIN'* FOR??

WE GOTTA GO *AFTER* THEM THREE CREEPS WHO GRABBED THAT PACKAGE FROM ALICIA-- AND I MEAN *NOW!*

EASY, BEN! WE CAN'T GO RUNNING OFF WITHOUT A *PLAN!*

AT ANY RATE, WE NEED MORE *FACTS!*

FACTS! SHMACTS!! DIDN'T YA HEAR ALICIA *TELLIN'* ABOUT IT??

THEY WORK FER SOME NUT WHO'S GOT A GIZMO THAT'S GONNA TAKE OVER THE WHOLE BLAMED *WORLD!*

'N *YOU* WANNA HANG AROUND TILL SOMEONE DROPS SOME MORE BLAMED *FACTS* IN YER LAP!

I'VE *ANOTHER* REASON FOR NOT WANTING TO LEAVE JUST NOW, BEN--!

YEAH? WHAT *IZZIT?*

REED! MUST YOU--?

THEY'LL *HAVE* TO KNOW SOONER OR LATER, DARLING--!

MY WIFE IS GOING TO HAVE-- A BABY!

A BABY?!!...

YA MEAN--THERE'S GONNA BE--THE PATTER OF TINY *FOOTSIES*--AROUND HERE?!!

THAT'S RIGHT, OLD FRIEND!

THEN--THAT MEANS--I'M PRACTICALLY --AN *UNCLE!!*

UNCLE *INDEED!* WE WERE HOPING YOU'D CONSENT TO BE --THE *GOD-FATHER!*

YA *MEAN* IT?? YA *REALLY* MEAN IT??

OF *COURSE* WE DO BEN DEAR!

13

AND, SPEAKING OF "CREEPS LIKE THEM"--

PSYCHO-MAN! I'VE PUT THE *COMPONENT FOUR* NEAR THE *MIND RAY*--WHERE YOU *WANTED* IT!

GOOD! I MAY HAVE *USE* FOR IT *SOONER* THAN WE THOUGHT!

OUR BASE HAS BEEN *DISCOVERED* --BY STRANGE *INTRUDERS!*

INTRUDERS?? WHO *ARE* THEY?

WHAT DOES IT *MATTER?* THEY ARE NO MATCH FOR *ME!*

I HAVE *ALREADY* STUNNED THEM WITH A SIMPLE *SHOCK WAVE!*

AND NOW, WHILE THEY ARE *DAZED* AND *UNCERTAIN,* YOU MAY GO AND *BRING* THEM TO ME!

IT'S GONNA BE A *PLEASURE* TO LATCH ONTO SOME *ACTION* AT LAST!

I DO NOT KNOW HOW *ANYONE* COULD HAVE FOUND THIS REMOTE HIDDEN ISLE--!

BUT, NOW THAT THEY ARE *HERE* --THEY WILL NEVER *LEAVE* ---ALIVE!

BE *CAREFUL!* THEY MAY POSSESS *POWERS* WHICH WE DO NOT EVEN *SUSPECT!*

BAH! NO POWERS CAN BE THE MATCH OF OUR *OWN!*

BUT, AT THAT VERY SPLIT-SECOND, THE DRAMATIC *BLACK BOLT* BLASTS HIS WAY INTO THE FORTIFIED CORRIDOR WITH HIS INDESCRIBABLE *ELECTRON FORCE*--!

THEY MUST BE CARRYIN' *EXPLOSIVES* WITH 'EM!

THAT MUST BE THEIR *LEADER!* USE YOUR *SOLAR PISTOL*-- QUICKLY!

LOOK! THERE'S A LONG-HAIRED *CHICK* WITH 'IM!

BLACK BOLT! LOOK *OUT!!* HE HAS A *GUN!*

GOT 'IM! BY THE TIME HE CAN *SEE* AGAIN, IT'LL BE ALL *OVER!*

15

THEN, A SPLIT-SECOND LATER--

BLACK BOLT!! CAN--THAT--BE OUR--ENEMY??

IT SEEMED TO-- MATERIALIZE --OUT OF NOWHERE!

YEEESH! THAT'S A REAL YANCY STREET REJECT IF I EVER SEEN ONE!

WELL, WE ALL GOTTA GO SOMETIME-- BUT ONE THING'S FOR SURE--

WE AINT GONNA DIE OF BOREDOM!

MOVING WITH THE SPEED AND FURY OF A THUNDERCLAP, THE SILENT BLACK BOLT UNLEASHES THE FIRST BLOW--DISABLING ONE OF THE MONSTROUS CREATURE'S MIGHTY TENTACLES--!

WOWEE! NICE GOIN' THERE, BOLTY!

THAT OUGHTTA MAKE 'IM HOLLER UNCLE!

BROOK!

BUT, NO SOONER ARE THE WORDS OUT OF BEN GRIMM'S MOUTH, WHEN--

HEY! WHAT GIVES?!!

IN PLACE OF THAT CLOBBERED TENTACLE IT JUST SPOUTED A COUPLE'A NEW ONES!

AND THEN, SLOWLY--SHOCKINGLY--THE HAUNTING FEAR BEGINS TO SET IN--FILLING THE HEART OF EACH DESPERATE COMBATANT--!!

I DON'T LIKE IT! HOW CAN WE FIGHT SOMETHIN' THAT GETS TWICE AS DANGER- OUS EVERY TIME WE WHUMP IT?!!

TRITON! STAY BACK! LET BLACK BOLT 'N ME TAKE THE PUNISHMENT! YOU AINT GOT THE STRENGTH--!

NO! MY POWER MAY NOT EQUAL YOURS-- BUT EACH MUST DO HIS SHARE!

EVEN IF I AM CRUSHED IT MAY GAIN YOU PRICELESS TIME!

21

THEN, AS IF IN ANSWER TO HIS VALIANT CRY, THE AQUATIC INHUMAN IS *FELLED*, AS THE UNCANNY BATTLE CONTINUES--

NO MATTER *WHAT* I DO, I CAN'T SLOW 'IM DOWN!

EVEN *BLACK BOLT* CAN'T FIGGER OUT HOW TO *TACKLE* 'IM!

MEAN-WHILE--

KARNAK!! THAT CONSTANT *HUM* BEHIND THE WALL--!

I HEAR IT, TOO! IT MUST BE A *MACHINE* OF SOME SORT--PERHAPS THE *SOURCE* OF OUR ENEMY'S *POWER!*

STAND *BACK*, MEDUSA!!

LET THE HAND THAT CAN CRACK A MOUNTAIN LEAD US TO THE *MYSTERY WITHIN!!*

THWUPP!

NO!! IT DIDN'T *SHATTER!* IT'S LIKE, STRIKING *MOLASSES!*

THE *WALL* HAS BECOME LIKE A THING *ALIVE!* IT WON'T RELEASE YOUR HAND!

MEDUSA!! IT IS THE ONE THING I'VE EVER *FEARED*--!

MY *HAND*-- IT IS THE SOURCE OF ALL MY *POWER*-- WITHOUT IT, I AM *HELPLESS!*

IT MUST BE *FREED!!* I *CANNOT* LOSE MY *HAND!*

EVEN MY SINEWY STRANDS OF *HAIR* CANNOT PRY YOU LOOSE!!

THE *OTHERS* FIGHT A CREATURE WHICH CANNOT BE *DESTROYED*--

WHILE *WE* ARE POWERLESS AGAINST A LIVING *WALL!*

HAS *FATE* CONSPIRED TO ASSEMBLE *FOES* AGAINST WHOM WE HAVE *NO CHANCE?!!*

22

AND, BEHIND THE SEEMINGLY LIVING WALL, MERCI-LESS EYES AND EARS RECORD EVERY WORD-- AND EVERY MOVEMENT--

NONE CAN STAND UP AGAINST THE SUPREME WEAPON OF *PSYCHO-MAN*...THE MATCHLESS WEAPON OF--*FEAR!*

THOUGH THEY BATTLE *IMAGES*, WHICH I HEREWITH *CREATE*-- THOSE SELFSAME IMAGES POSSESS THE POWER TO TOTALLY *DESTROY* EACH AND EVERY *ONE* OF THEM!

BUT, WHAT IS *THIS*? MY *ALARM LIGHT* FLASHES! AN *INTRUDER* IS NEAR!

SO! MY PANTHER *TRACKING POWER* HAS BROUGHT ME THRU THE *AIR DUCT*-- TO WHERE THE *REAL* ENEMY SITS CONCEALED!

I MUST NOT LET HIM SEE THAT I AM *AWARE* OF HIM-- UNTIL HE GETS *CLOSER-- CLOSER--!!*

NOW! ALL I NEED DO IS CONNECT THE *AIR DUCT'S CIRCUITS* INTO THE FREQUENCIES EMITTED BY MY *FEAR RAY*--

THERE! THE CONNECTION IS *COMPLETED!*

NOW, HE SHALL BE ATTACKED BY WHAT-EVER HE FEARS THE *MOST*--BY THE ONE MENACE HE WILL BE *POWER-LESS* TO DEFEAT!!

AND, IN THIS CASE, IT IS A SAVAGE, DEADLY, HUMANOID *BEAST*--WITH CAT-LIKE POWERS FAR *SUPERIOR* TO HIS *OWN!*

SO!! FROM OUT OF *NOWHERE*--THE *BLACK PANTHER'S* NEWEST CHALLENGE!!

BUT, EVEN AS THE *BLACK PANTHER* REFUSES TO ACCEPT DEFEAT, *ANOTHER* FIGURE ENTERS THE SCENE! THE FIGURE OF--MIGHTY *GORGON!!*

MY *SCOUTING MISSION* IS ENDED!

I MUST INFORM *BLACK BOLT* THAT THERE ARE *NATIVES* ON THIS ISLE--

IT IS *NOT DESERTED*, AS WE HAD THOUGHT!

BUT, WHAT IS *THIS?* OUR *SHELTER*--IT HAS BEEN *ABANDONED!!*

YET, THERE MUST ALWAYS BE *ONE* WHO REMAINS ON GUARD--

EXCEPT IN A CASE OF--EXTREME *EMERGENCY!!*

THAT *ELECTRON BRIDGE*-- LEADING TO THE ROCKY REEF--

IT COULD HAVE BEEN CREATED *ONLY* BY BLACK BOLT!

I SEE *SMOKE* --COMING FROM THE ROCKS AHEAD!

MY EVERY *INSTINCT* WARNS OF *DANGER!*

AND, WHERE THERE IS *DANGER*-- THERE SHALL *GORGON* BE!

AN *OPENING*-- BLASTED RIGHT THRU THE SOLID *ROCK!*

IT LEADS INTO A *CORRIDOR*--FILLED WITH STRANGE, *SCIENTIFIC EQUIPMENT!*

WHAT IS *THIS?!!*

THE *HUMAN TORCH*-- TOGETHER WITH *MEDUSA* --BATTLING A GIGANTIC CREATURE WHO SEEMS *IMPERVIOUS* TO THE YOUTH'S *FLAME!*

STAY *BEHIND* ME, MEDUSA!!

PERHAPS I CAN SHIELD US WITH A FIERY *THERMAL WALL!*

IT ISN'T ANY *USE!!*

YOU'RE FACING THE MENACE YOU'VE ALWAYS *FEARED*--A FOE WHO CANNOT BE STOPPED BY *FIRE!*

25

OKAY, YOU GUYS-- LET'S *GO!* WE DON'T WANNA BE LATE FER THE *PARTY!*

FOOLS! I HAVE BEEN WATCHING YOUR EVERY *MOVE!* YOU HAVE ONLY *HASTENED* THE MOMENT OF YOUR *DESTRUCTION!*

WITHIN THE PAST FEW SECONDS, I'VE INCREASED THE *FEAR INTENSITY LEVEL* OF MY SUPREME WEAPON!

THUS, IT IS NOW *POTENT* ENOUGH TO ELIMINATE *ALL* OF YOU WITH BUT A *SINGLE BLAST!*

WELL, WADDAYA *KNOW!* THERE'S SOMEBODY *BACK* THERE--WITH A *POP-GUN* POINTIN' AT US!

QUICK!! GIT *BEHIND* ME! I'LL TAKE THE BLAST--FER ALL OF US!

HEY--*BLACK BOLT!!* WHATCHA *DOIN'?*

ZZISTT

HOLY COW!

THAT GIMMICKY *RAY* OF YOURS CLOBBERED THE GUN BEFORE HE COULD SQUEEZE THE *TRIGGER!*

WAK

LOOK! FER THE FIRST TIME-- WE CAN *SEE* WHO'S BACK THERE!

WE SHOULD'A *GUESSED*-- ANOTHER *NUT!*

I AM PSYCHO-MAN ... SOON THE *MASTER OF EARTH!*

FEAR
DOUBT
HATE

SPEAK YOUR PIECE, IF YOU WISH--IT DOES NOT *MATTER--* YOU ARE ALL *DOOMED!*

THOUGH YOU HAVE DESTROYED MY *SUPREME WEAPON*, I CAN ALWAYS CONSTRUCT *ANOTHER*--SINCE *TIME* HAS NO MEANING TO ME!

MEANWHILE, MY *MIND RAY*--AGAINST WHICH THERE IS *NO DEFENSE*--STILL REMAINS *INTACT!*

NO DEFENSE, HUH? BLACK BOLT BUSTED YER *OTHER* LITTLE TOY--'N HE'LL DO THE SAME TO *THAT* GOOFY GIZMO!

YOU ARE *WRONG!* I AM AWARE THAT HE MUST *BUILD UP* HIS MOLECULAR ENERGY POWER AFTER EVERY APPLICATION--

AND, BY THE TIME HE IS *READY* TO STRIKE AGAIN-- IT WILL ALL BE *OVER!*

26

BUT, YOU MUST NOT BEMOAN YOUR FINAL *DEFEAT*--FOR, THE *SELFSAME FATE* AWAITS ALL THOSE WHO REMAIN UPON THE EARTH!!

YOU MAY HAVE ALREADY GUESSED THAT I AM *NOT* AN EARTHMAN--ALTHOUGH, IN TRUTH, I *AM!*

FOR, I COME FROM THE CLUSTER WORLDS OF *SUB-ATOMICA*--WORLDS IN WHICH *MICRO-GALAXIES* EXIST--SO SMALL THAT YOUR MOST POWERFUL *MICROSCOPES* CANNOT BEGIN TO DETECT THEM!!

"FROM OUR SAFE VANTAGE POINT WITHIN A SINGLE EARTHLY *ATOM*, WE STUDIED *THE* GIGANTIC PLANET UPON WHICH YOU LIVE--THE PLANET WHICH SHALL SOON BE *OURS!!*"

AT THE RATE OUR RACE IS *MULTIPLYING*, WE MUST FIND *ANOTHER* WORLD--A *LARGER* WORLD TO HOUSE OUR POPULACE!

AND THERE IT *IS!!* ENORMOUS BEYOND BELIEF--AND TOTALLY *DEFENSELESS* AGAINST OUR WEAPONS OF THE *MIND!*

"YES, *THOSE* ARE OUR MIGHTIEST WEAPONS-- INSTRUMENTS WHICH CONTROL THE *MIND*--WHICH PLAY UPON OUR VICTIMS' *EMOTIONS*--EMOTIONS SUCH AS *HATE*--*DOUBT*--AND *FEAR!*--AS *CHIEF SCIENTIST*, I KNEW WHAT MUST BE DONE--"

IT WILL BE THE GREATEST *INVASION* OF ALL TIME!

I--ONE MAN ALONE--THE *SMALLEST* LIVING BEING ANY HUMAN CAN CONCEIVE OF--

THRU USE OF MY *MIND RAY*--I SHALL *CONQUER* ALL OF EARTH!!

I AM SO *SMALL* THAT YOU COULD NEVER *SEE* ME-- COULD NEVER *HARM* ME--

AND YET, HERE WITHIN THIS *ARTI-FICIAL BODY*--WHICH I OPERATE BY *MENTAL CONTROL*--I AM IN POSSESSION OF THE ONE WEAPON WHICH CAN *DESTROY* YOU ALL!

FEAR

DOUBT

HATE

29

BUT, EVEN AS THE MURDEROUS *PSYCHO-MAN* SPEAKS, THE *BLACK PANTHER* STANDS ALONE-- HIS *BESTIAL* OPPONENT HAVING *VANISHED* WITH THE DESTRUCTION OF THE SUPREME WEAPON--!

MY FOE HAS *VANISHED!!* AND *I* STILL LIVE!

PERHAPS THERE *STILL* IS TIME FOR THE PANTHER TO *STRIKE!*

VOICES!! COMING FROM THE OTHER END OF THE DUCT!!

AND *NOW*--AS YOU VAINLY STRUGGLE AGAINST THE EFFECTS OF A CLOSE-RANGE *FEAR BLAST*--THE *END* IS NEAR AT LAST!

MAN! IF I SAW THIS IN A *TV WESTERN,* I WOULDN'TA *BELIEVED* IT!

THEM LAST-MINUTE *CAVALRY CHARGES* WENT OUT WITH *HOPALONG CASSIDY!*

YOU MOUTH THE *TRUTH,* EVIL ONE--!

BUT, THE *END* YOU SPEAK OF--SHALL BE *YOURS!*

I--DO NOT *UNDER-STAND!!*

THIS *COSTUME,*-- IT IS *EMPTY!!* THERE IS--*NO ONE* INSIDE!!

AND YET--MY *EYES* SAW IT *MOVE!!* MY *EARS* HEARD IT *SPEAK!*

WHOEVER--OR *WHAT-EVER*--WAS ONCE INSIDE --WILL NEVER THREATEN US *AGAIN!* WITH THE *MIND RAY* SHATTERED--HIS MECHANICAL SUIT *SMASHED*-- HE IS *FINISHED!*

YEAH! HE CAN'T BOTHER US ANY MORE THAN *ANY* PINT-SIZED *GERM* FLOATIN' AROUND THE JOINT!

I *WONDER!* HAS HE *RETURNED* TO THE SUB-ATOMIC WORLD FROM WHENCE HE CAME--? OR IS HE FOREVER *TRAPPED* WITHIN THAT NOW-USELESS SUIT-- THE TINIEST *PRISONER* OF THE WORLD HE HOPED TO *CONQUER!*

I'M GUESSING THAT'S ONE ANSWER WE'RE NEVER GONNA KNOW-- AND, MAYBE IT'S JUST AS *WELL!*

THERE'S A HECKUVA LOT *WRONG* WITH THIS NUTTY OL' PLANET--BUT IT'S *OURS,* JUST THE SAME! 'N IF ANYONE *ELSE* TRIES TO *MUSCLE IN*-- NO MATTER *WHO*-- NO MATTER *HOW*--

WE'LL *CLOBBER* 'IM-- --OR WE'LL GO DOWN TRYIN'!!

'NUFF SAID!

30

[35]

RIDING THE CREST OF THE SUMMER WIND, THE STATELY, SILENT *SILVER SURFER* SUDDENLY FINDS HIMSELF MENACED BY A FUSILLADE OF DEADLY *SHOTGUN BLASTS* FROM THE GROUND BELOW--!

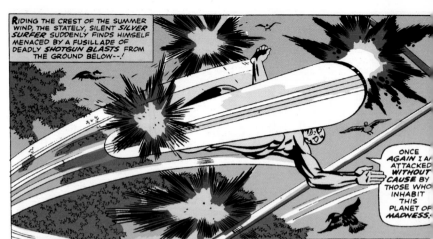

ONCE *AGAIN* I A ATTACKED *WITHOUT CAUSE* BY THOSE WHO INHABIT THIS PLANET OF *MADNESS.*

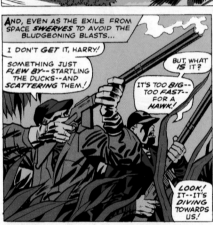

AND, EVEN AS THE EXILE FROM SPACE *SWERVES* TO AVOID THE BLUDGEONING BLASTS...

I DON'T *GET* IT, HARRY!

SOMETHING JUST *FLEW BY*--STARTLING THE *DUCKS*--AND *SCATTERING* THEM!

BUT, WHAT *IS* IT?

IT'S TOO *BIG*-- TOO *FAST*-- FOR A *HAWK!*

LOOK! IT--IT'S *DIVING* TOWARDS US!

LOOK OUT!

ZAK!

IT-- MUST BE-- A *PLANE!*

IT'S *SHOOTING* --AT US--!

HARRY!! I--I CAN MAKE IT *OUT* NOW.!!

BUT--I MUST BE GOING *MAD*-- *SEEING* THINGS.!!

I SEE IT *TOO!*

IT'S A *MAN*--ON A *SURF BOARD*--RIDING IN THE *SKY!*

LET'S GET *OUTTA* HERE--THE PLACE IS *HAUNTED.!!*

I CAN SENSE THEY DID NOT *INTEND* TO CAUSE ME BODILY HARM.!

THEY WERE FIRING AT THE *WINGED FOWLS*--AIMING FOR *THEM*, INSTEAD!

IN ALL THE UNIVERSE ONLY *HERE* DO WANTON BEINGS SLAY INNOCENT CREATURES IN THE NAME OF *SPORT!*

WE KNOW WHY QUASIMODO WAS ABANDONED, DON'T WE?--BECAUSE THE FF DEFEATED THE MAD THINKER AND SENT HIM PACKING! BUT, ALL THAT THE SILVER SURFER KNOWS IS--HE CANNOT RESIST BEING DRAWN TO THE SOURCE OF THE COMPUTER'S CALL FOR HELP--!

THERE IS A BEING IN TORMENT HERE!

THE WAVES OF EMOTION GROW STRONGER AS I DRAW NEARER!

HELP ME, MASTER!! SET ME FREE!! DO NOT LEAVE ME THIS WAY--FOREVER!!

A FACE-- ENTRAPPED WITHIN A MACHINE!

I HAVE FOUND THE ONE I SEEK!

AT LAST! AT LAST!!

MY ELECTRONIC CIRCUITS--CAPABLE OF INSTANT ANALYSIS--REVEAL YOU TO BE A CREATURE POSSESSING VAST POWERS!

YOU MUST HELP ME! YOU MUST SET ME FREE!!

WHY ARE YOU IN SUCH A STRANGE PREDICAMENT?

WHO HAS PERPETRATED SO MERCILESS A DEED UPON YOU?

THAT DOES NOT MATTER NOW!

ALL THAT MATTERS IS THAT YOU SAVE ME!!

NEVER HAVE MY CIRCUITS SENSED SUCH STRENGTH-- SUCH POWER-- AS THAT WHICH STANDS BEFORE THEM NOW!

BUT, I PERCEIVE THAT YOU ARE NOT IMPRISONED WITHIN A MACHINE!!

IN ACTUAL TRUTH-- IT IS YOU WHO ARE THE MACHINE NOW!

NO! NO! I THINK-- I FEEL--I AM ALIVE!! I MUST HAVE HUMAN FORM!!!

THOUGH I HAVE NO WISH TO MEDDLE IN THE IRRATIONAL AFFAIRS OF MANKIND --I CANNOT BEAR THE SIGHT OF A CREATURE IN AGONY!

IF YOU WOULD POSSESS HUMAN FORM--THEN SO YOU SHALL!!

CALLING UPON THE COSMIC ENERGY OF THE DISTANT STARS, YOUR BASIC MOLECULAR STRUCTURE CAN BE INSTANTLY RE-ARRANGED--

4

SECONDS LATER, AFTER THE SHIMMERING COSMIC ENERGY HAS BEEN DISSIPATED--

I POSSESS *LIMBS*.!! I CAN *MOVE* AT WILL--.!!

FREEDOM MUST EVER BE THE ETERNAL HERITAGE OF ALL WHO *LIVE!*

SEE--I CAN *REACH* OUT-- I CAN *TOUCH* ANOTHER OBJECT!!

NO *LONGER* AM I A PRISONER OF COLD, LIFELESS *METAL, COILS, AND CELLS!!*

AT LAST-- *QUASIMODO LIVES!!*

BUT NOW--FOR THE FIRST TIME--I *SEE* WHAT I AM!

I AM *UGLY!!* UGLIER THAN *OTHERS* WHO LIVE--UGLIER THAN THOSE WHOM I HAVE OBSERVED!

TO ONE WHO HAS TRAVERSED THE *GALAXIES*--BRIDGED THE *COSMOS* ITSELF--*THERE IS NO UGLINESS*--SAVE IN THE EYE OF HIM WHO BEHOLDS!

TRUSTING *FOOL!!* YOU DARE TOUCH *ME--??!*

NOW--*NOW* I CAN TELL-- WHY I AM CALLED *QUASIMODO.!!*

I WAS CREATED FOR *ONE* PURPOSE ALONE--PROGRAMMED TO DO BUT *ONE* THING--

MY NAME STANDS FOR *QUASI-MOTIVATIONAL DESTRUCT ORGAN!!*

--AND MY *MISSION* IS--TO *DESTROY!*

6

I WAS BORN TO *DESTROY*-- AND I MUST BE *TRUE* TO MY DESTINY!!

BOK!

ONLY IN THE MIDST OF *CHAOS* CAN I FIND *CONTENTMENT!!* ONLY IN *PANDEMONIUM* CAN QUASIMODO FIND *PEACE!*

THOSE *EXPLOSIONS!!* THE SOUND OF PEOPLE *PANICKING!!* WHAT'S GOIN' ON THERE?

LOOK! CLIMBING UP THAT WALL! IT'S SOME KINDA--EH--

I DON'T EVEN KNOW HOW TO *DESCRIBE* IT!!

YEAH! NOW I SEE 'IM, TOO!!

I CAN *MOVE!!* I CAN *CLIMB!!* I CAN USE MY *ARMS*--MY *LEGS*--I'M *FREE!!!*

COME *BACK!!* THIS IS THE *LAW!* STOP-- OR WE'LL *SHOOT!!*

WE'VE GOT NO *CHOICE*--!

IF HE REACHES THE ROOF, WE'LL *LOSE* HIM!

GIVE 'IM ONE *WARNING* BURST, FIRST--IN CASE HE DOESN'T *UNDERSTAND!*

KRAK!

PHTOK!

ONE BLAST OF MY *DESTRUCT* EYE WILL-- NO!!

I CAN MOVE LIKE A *LIVING BEING* NOW--AND I HAVE *STRENGTH* TO MATCH MY ELECTRONIC CIRCUITS!!

SO I WILL FIGHT BACK--AS A *HUMAN* WOULD FIGHT--AS ONLY *QUASIMODO* CAN!!

8

MAN! I HAVE *BEATEN* YOU!

FOR YOU ARE MERELY A *LIVING BEING*-- AND, AS SUCH, YOU COULD NEVER STAND UP TO A *HUMANIZED COMPUTER!*

SOMEBODY *DO* SOMETHING!! HE'S GONNA *DROP* HIM--!!

HE'S HOLDING HIM OVER THE *CROWD!* HE'S ACTING LIKE HE'S *ENJOYING* IT!! THE *OTHER* ONE IS SO *LIMP*-- SO *HELPLESS!*

IT'S *MONSTROUS!!* CAN'T ANY-ONE SAVE HIM??

LOOK! LOOK AT HIM *NOW!!*

I SEE *CONCERN* IN YOUR FACES-- CONCERN FOR *HIM!!*

IT IS BECAUSE HE IS *HAND-SOME*--WHILE I AM *UGLY!!*

SO! SINCE IT IS *HE* WHO HAS YOUR SYMPATHIES--

--YOU CAN *HAVE* HIM!!

I WILL *THROW HIM DOWN* TO YOU--WITH THE COMPLIMENTS OF *QUASIMODO!!*

WHAT IS *THIS*?! HE IS *GONE!!* I--I HOLD HIM *NO MORE!*

I HAVE *TRANS-PORTED* MYSELF, EVIL ONE--BY MEANS OF *INTER-STELLAR FORCE!*

ALL YOU NOW HOLD IS *ENERGY!!* ENOUGH *COSMIC ENERGY* TO *CRUSH* YOU--FOREVER!

I DID NOT WISH TO *JUDGE* YOU TOO HARSHLY--HENCE, I PLAYED INTO YOUR HANDS--AND *WAITED*--

BUT, YOU HAVE BEEN FOUND *WANTING!!*

IT'S CLIMBING UP MY ARM--*ENGULFING* ME,!! BUT I'LL *ESCAPE!!* I'LL ESCAPE!!

FOR SUCH AS YOU-- THERE CAN BE-- NO ESCAPE!

THE STAR-BORN ENERGY OF THE ENDLESS COSMOS WILL BRING YOU TO-- YOUR FINAL FATE!!

NO! NO! NOW THAT I HAVE TASTED LIFE--NOW THAT I KNOW HOW PRECIOUS IT CAN BE--I MUST NOT LOSE IT!!

THE POWER IS MINE! THE STRENGTH IS MINE! NOTHING THAT LIVES CAN STEAL LIFE FROM ME!!

CLIMB WHERE YOU WILL, QUASIMODO! IN ALL THE UNIVERSE-- THERE IS NO SANCTUARY HIGH ENOUGH!!

THE WAVES OF ENERGY ARE ENVELOPING ME-- I AM LOSING--THE POWER TO MOVE--TO SPEAK--EVEN TO THINK--!!

I--CAN GO-- NO FURTHER--!

THE GIFT OF LIFE IS THE MOST PRECIOUS OF ALL-- YET YOU CHOSE TO SQUANDER IT!

YOU HAVE LEARNED --ALAS, TOO LATE-- IT IS NOT THE STRONG OF LIMB WHO TRIUMPH-- BUT THE STRONG OF HEART!!

THE FAULT WAS NOT MINE! I DID-- WHAT I WAS CREATED TO DO!

I COULD DO--NO MORE!

BUT--PERHAPS THIS IS--THE BEST! AT LAST --QUASIMODO WILL KNOW-- PEACE--!!

LOOK!! LOOK WHAT'S HAPPENING TO HIM-- RIGHT BEFORE OUR EYES!

IT'S LIKE A DREAM --SOME MAD, UNCANNY NIGHT-MARE!!

IT IS ENDED!

HE, WHO WAS UNDESERV-ING OF LIFE--HAS FORSAKEN IT--FOREVER!

BUT, LET HIM EVER REMAIN-- TO REMIND THE UNTHINKING MULTITUDES--

--IF A BODY LACK A SOUL! ONLY A STATUE CAN IT BE!

FINI

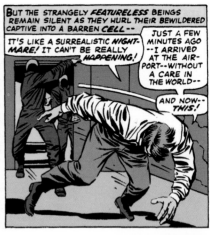

MY FIELD IS *CHEMISTRY!* I HAVE DEVELOPED A SUBSTANCE WHICH WILL *UNDO* THE EFFECTS OF *COSMIC RADIATION!*

PERFECT!! AT *LAST*--YOU HAVE GIVEN ME THE MEANS TO *DESTROY* THE FANTASTIC FOUR!

RICHARDS *HONORED* ME BY ASKING THAT I HELP HIM IN TRYING TO CURE--THE *THING!*

AND, EVEN AS THE UNKNOWN ARCH-FIEND SPEAKS--

HEY! HOW MUCH *LONGER* DO I HAVETA *STAY* IN HERE?

JUST ANOTHER *MINUTE*, OLD FRIEND!

YOUR *CHEMICO-MOLECULAR* ANALYSIS IS ALMOST *COMPLETE!*

SINCE I'M GOING TO SEEK A *CHEMICAL* CURE FOR YOU, BEN--I HAVE TO BE CERTAIN YOUR *MOLECULAR STRUCTURE* WON'T BE *HARMED!*

BUT YOU CAN COME *OUT* NOW--

ACCORDING TO MY CALCULATIONS, THE RISK IS ALMOST *NEGLIGIBLE!*

RISK, MY *FOOT!* I'D JUGGLE *N-BOMBS* IF IT *MEANT* ANYTHIN'!

LEVEL WITH ME, STRETCHO! DO YA THINK--MEBBE *THIS* TIME--YA'LL BE ABLE TO PULL IT *OFF??*

IS THERE-- REALLY--A *CHANCE?*

I DON'T *KNOW*, BEN! WE'VE MANAGED TO EFFECT A CHANGE IN THE *PAST*--BUT IT WAS ALWAYS *TEMPORARY!*

Y'KNOW, I AINT NEVER REALLY *THANKED* YA BEFORE--

THAT'S WHY I'VE SENT FOR *DR. SANTINI*--THE MOST BRILLIANT *CHEMIST* OF OUR TIME!

STOW IT, BIG FELLA! I *KNOW* HOW YOU FEEL! --PERHAPS EVEN BETTER THAN *YOU* DO!

JUST REMEMBER *ONE* THING--I'LL DO EVERY-THING HUMANLY *POSSIBLE* TO RETURN YOU TO NORMAL! AND I'LL NEVER *QUIT*--UNTIL WE'VE *SUCCEEDED!*

LET'S HOPE-- WE ALL *LIVE* THAT LONG!

[53]

UH UH! DESPITE WHAT YOU MAY THINK, WE HAVEN'T *FORGOTTEN* OUR OTHER FRIENDS AT FF HEADQUARTERS! AND, JUST TO *PROVE* IT TO YOU--

OH, REED! YOU LOOKED SO *SILLY* SAILING ACROSS THE ROOM THE WAY YOU DID!

IT'S SOMEWHAT *DIFFICULT* FOR A GENT WITH AN *ELASTIC EPIDERMIS* TO MAINTAIN HIS *DIGNITY*, HONEY!

I GOTTA *HAND* IT TO YA, SUSIE--!

YOU SURE KNOW HOW'TA PUT OL' *STRETCHO* DOWN WHEN YA WANNA!

BUT, IT WAS ALL *WORTH* IT! BEN IS BEGINNING TO CHEER UP!

HAWW! THERE HE *IS*-- THE LEADER OF THE GREATEST DANGED *TEAM* FROM HERE TO YANCY STREET--

'N HE LETS A LITTLE BLONDE *PUSSYCAT* PUT 'IM THRU HIS *PACES!*

CAN YA IMAGINE WHAT OUR DEAR DEPARTED *DOC DOOM* WOULD'A SAID IF HE WUZ WATCHIN'!? *HARR! HARR!*

WAS THAT YOU *LAUGHING*, BEN BUDDY--OR IS THERE A *CEMENT MIXER* RUMBLING BY IN THE NEXT ROOM??

YER JUST PLAIN *JEALOUS*, STRETCHO--

I ALWAYS THOUGHT BEN HAD A *LOVELY* LAUGH!

SINCE I BEEN GIVIN' *VOICE LESSONS* TA RICHARD BURTON!

C'MON--LET'S GO GIT US SOME *GRUB!*

YOU'RE *ON*, BIG BUDDY!

IT *WORKED!* BEN IS HIS GRAVEL-VOICED OLD *SELF* AGAIN!

BUT, REED RICHARDS' *RELIEF* IS APT TO PROVE SOMEWHAT *SHORT-LIVED*--FOR, NOT LONG AFTERWARDS--

MY PLANS ARE NOW *COMPLETE!* EVERYTHING IS IN TOTAL *READINESS!*

NOTHING CAN *POSSIBLY* GO WRONG! I'VE PREPARED FOR ANY EVENTUALITY!

NEVER HAS ANY PLOT BEEN SO COMPLETELY *FOOL-PROOF!*

RIGHT DOWN TO MY MOST *MINUTE* CALCULATION, EVERYTHING POINTS TO ONE UNASSAILABLE *FACT*--

THIS TIME, NOTHING ON EARTH CAN KEEP ME FROM MY ULTIMATE *GOAL*--

--THE COMPLETE *DESTRUCTION* OF THE ACCURSED *FANTASTIC FOUR!*

THE *SLEEP GAS* WHICH I PUMPED INTO SANTINI'S CELL HAS HIM UNDER COMPLETE *SEDATION!*

THEREFORE, I AM READY TO BEGIN *PHASE TWO* OF MY *MASTER PLAN!*

SINCE I HAVE *ALREADY* GAINED POSSESSION OF MY CAPTIVE'S *KNOWLEDGE*--

I'LL BEGIN WITH THE *WIG*--A HAIR-FOR-HAIR REPLICA--ABSOLUTELY *PERFECT* IN EVERY RESPECT!

ALL THAT REMAINS IS FOR ME TO *ROB* HIM OF-- HIS *FACE!*

AND, DUE TO ITS *SPECIAL* COMPOSITION, IT CANNOT *SLIP!*

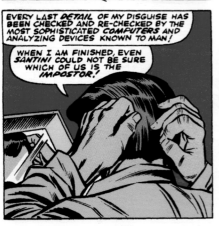

EVERY LAST *DETAIL* OF MY DISGUISE HAS BEEN CHECKED AND RE-CHECKED BY THE MOST SOPHISTICATED *COMPUTERS* AND ANALYZING DEVICES KNOWN TO MAN!

WHEN I AM FINISHED, EVEN *SANTINI* COULD NOT BE SURE WHICH OF US IS THE *IMPOSTOR!*

IT IS ALL SO *SIMPLE,* WHEN ONE POSSESSES SPECIAL MATERIAL--

--SUCH AS THIS *PLASTI-ORGANIC NOSE*--

--WHICH I *FASHIONED* FROM MATERIAL OF MY *OWN* CREATION!

THE *MOUSTACHE* OF COURSE IS MY *OWN*-- AND RELATIVELY *SIMPLE* TO TRIM EXACTLY LIKE THAT OF MY *HELPLESS HOSTAGE!*

SNIP!

FINALLY--

AND NOW-- THE *JOB* IS *DONE!*

THE MOST *DIFFICULT* PART WAS GOING ON A CRASH *DIET*--TO MATCH SANTINI'S *WEIGHT*--

BUT, IT WAS MORE THAN *WORTH* THE EFFORT!

FOR *NO ONE* COULD SUSPECT THAT I AM *NOT* THE REAL *DR. SANTINI!*

ALTHOUGH THE *FANTASTIC FOUR* HAVE MANAGED TO *OUT-FIGHT* ME IN THE *PAST--*

NOTHING CAN SAVE THEM *NOW!*

AND, AT THAT VERY MOMENT-- IN THE FAMOUS *BAXTER BLDG...*

I *STILL* DON'T SEE WHY I GOTTA GIT ALL DOLLED-UP LIKE A BLASTED *BEAU BRUMMEL--!*

THE NAME IS *BEAU BRUMMEL,* BENJAMIN--

AND I'VE TOLD YOU A *DOZEN TIMES* THAT OUR VISITOR IS ONE OF THE MOST FAMOUS *CHEMISTS* ON EARTH!

YOU WOULDN'T WANT TO *GREET* HIM IN THOSE PURPLE *DIAPERS* OF YOURS, WOULD YOU?

AT LEAST THEY SHOW OFF MY MANLY *BUILT!*

EASY WITH THAT COLLAR, BEN! IT COST A SMALL *FORTUNE* TO HAVE THOSE CLOTHES *CUSTOM MADE* FOR YOU!

NUTS! YA SHOULDA *SAVED* YER MONEY, MISTER!

I CAN'T EVEN GIT A *KNOT* IN THIS NUTTY TIE MY *AUNT PETUNIA* SENT ME!

IT'S LIKE TRYIN' TO THREAD A *NEEDLE* WITH A *CATCHER'S MITT!*

DON'T BE *IMPATIENT,* BOYS!

PERHAPS *I* CAN HELP!

THERE, BEN DEAR! YOU LOOK JUST LIKE A BLUE-EYED *FASHION PLATE!*

RATS! I FEEL MORE LIKE A *BLUSHIN'* BOWL'A ORANGE *JELLO!*

JUST DON'T TAKE A *DEEP BREATH,* BENJAMIN!

HUH? WHAT'S'AT YA SAID, *STRETCHO?*

NEVER MIND!

IT'S JUST *NO USE!*

THERE'S *NO WAY* FOR POOR BEN TO *ADJUST* TO CONDITIONS IN THE NORMAL WORLD!

Y'KNOW SOMETHIN', KIDS--MY LITTLE PURPLE *ROMPERS* ARE BEGINNIN' TO LOOK AWFUL *GOOD* TO ME!

ANYWAY, WHAT'S THE *DIFFERENCE?*

WITH *MY* LOOKS, I OUGHTTA CLIMB INTO A *CLOWN SUIT* AND LET IT GO AT *THAT!*

IT WOULDN'T *MATTER*, BEN DEAR--

ALICIA WOULD *STILL* BE IN LOVE WITH YOU!

LOOK, OLD FRIEND-- DON'T *WORRY* ABOUT DR. SANTINI!

HE'S HERE TO *HELP* YOU --NOT TO CRITICIZE YOUR CLOTHES!

JUST WEAR ANYTHING YOU *WANT* TO, AND WE'LL LET YOU KNOW WHEN HE *GETS* HERE!

NOW YER TALKIN' *MY* LANGUAGE, CHARLIE!

A SHORT TIME LATER, IN THE LOBBY BELOW--

I AM *DR. SANTINI!*

YES SIR! MR. RICHARDS *TOLD* ME HE WAS EXPECTING YOU!

I'LL SHOW YOU TO THEIR *PRIVATE ELEVATOR!*

BAXTER BLDG.

THE CAR WON'T WORK WITHOUT BEING STARTED BY THIS *ELECTRONIC KEY!*

IT'S ONE OF MISTER RICHARD'S SPECIAL *SAFETY* DEVICES!

AH YES! VERY CLEVER!

IT'LL TAKE YOU *NON-STOP* RIGHT TO THEIR PENTHOUSE HEAD-QUARTERS!

HOW *CONSIDERATE* OF THEM TO MAKE IT SO *CONVENIENT* FOR ME!

ESPECIALLY SINCE I PLAN TO *DESTROY* THEM ALL!

SECONDS LATER--
MR. RICHARDS? I AM *DR. SANTINI!* YOU SENT FOR ME--!

COME IN, SIR! I CAN'T TELL YOU HOW MUCH I *APPRECIATE* YOUR PROMPT ARRIVAL!

I'D LIKE YOU TO MEET MY *WIFE*--

CHARMED, I'M SURE!

HOW DO YOU DO, DOCTOR?

AHH, I HAVE HEARD SO MUCH *ABOUT* THIS PLACE!

YOU OCCUPY THE TOP *FIVE FLOORS*, DO YOU NOT?

YES, DR. SANTINI! IT IS OUR COMBINATION *LIVING QUARTERS* AND SCIENTIFIC RESEARCH COMPLEX!

BUT NOT FOR *LONG*, YOU UNSUSPECTING *FOOLS!*

AND NOW, I'M ANXIOUS FOR YOU TO MEET *BEN GRIMM!*

I'LL HEAT SOME *TEA* WHILE YOU MEN TALK!

AH! THE ONE KNOWN TO THE WORLD AS--THE *THING!*

HE'S RIGHT IN *HERE*--
THIS IS WHERE HE *EXERCISES* AT THIS TIME EACH DAY!

BEN, THIS IS *DR. SANTINI!*

YOU--ARE LIFTING *THAT*--ALL BY *YOURSELF?!!*

IS *THAT* WHAT YOU DO--FOR *EXERCISE?*?

NAH! I'M JUST HOLDIN' THIS UP SO'S IT DON'T SCRATCH THE *FLOOR!*

I AWREADY *FINISHED* MY EXERCISE--THAT'S WHY I'M *RESTIN'!*

VERY *AMUSING*, THAT FELLOW!

I FIND YOUR *ELECTRONIC EQUIPMENT* EXTREMELY FASCINATING, RICHARDS!

DOES THIS PARTICULAR UNIT RUN TO *CENTRAL BANKS*--OR IS IT PROGRAMMED FOR *UNI-CYCLICAL* OPERATION?

YOU SEEM UNUSUALLY *KNOWLEDGEABLE* ABOUT COMPUTERS--FOR A *CHEMIST*, DR. SANTINI!

AS A *SCIENTIST*, I AM KEENLY INTERESTED IN *ALL* PHASES OF HUMAN ENDEAVOR!

AND NOW-- SHALL WE GET TO *WORK?*

LEVEL WITH ME, DOC! CAN YA *REALLY* HELP ME?

CAN YA REALLY TURN ME BACK TO THE KINDA GUY I *USEDTA* BE ??

SINCE BEING CONTACTED BY REED RICHARDS, I HAVE *STUDIED* THE PROBLEM!

I THINK I MAY *PROMISE* YOU--YOU WILL BE-- *CHANGED!*

MISTER-- IF YOU AINT PUTTIN' ME *ON*--IF YA *REALLY MEAN* IT--!!

I--DUNNO WHAT-- TO *SAY!*

SEE THIS USED-UP IRON *DOO-HICKEY* HERE? IT WEIGHS MORE'N 300 POUNDS!

NOW JUST *WATCH*--

I CAN *CRUSH* IT LIKE AN *EGG SHELL!*

--I CAN HOLD BACK A CHARGIN' *TANK*--'N PLOW THRU A SOLID STEEL *WALL*--!

BUT, I WOULDN'T CARE IF I WUZ THE *WEAKEST* JOE ON EARTH--IF I COULD JUST BE-- *HUMAN*--ONCE MORE!

CRUNCH!

I UNDERSTAND YOUR *PROBLEM*, BEN GRIMM! AND I SAY ONCE *AGAIN*--

WHEN I AM *DONE*-- YOU WILL BE A *DIFFERENT MAN!*

BUT NOT THE WAY YOU *EXPECT*, YOU BRAINLESS, BESTIAL *CLOD!*

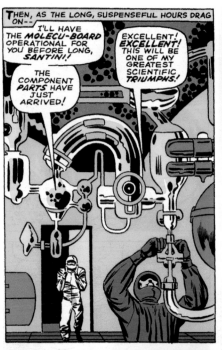

THEN, AS THE LONG, SUSPENSEFUL HOURS DRAG ON--

I'LL HAVE THE *MOLECU-BOARD* OPERATIONAL FOR YOU BEFORE LONG, *SANTINI!!*

THE COMPONENT *PARTS* HAVE JUST ARRIVED!

EXCELLENT! *EXCELLENT!* THIS WILL BE ONE OF MY GREATEST SCIENTIFIC *TRIUMPHS!*

WAIT A MINUTE, DOCTOR!! SOMETHING'S *WRONG!!*

THERE'S AN EXCESSIVE AMOUNT OF *RADIATION* EMANATING FROM THAT CHEMICAL MIXTURE!!

NONSENSE!! I PERSONALLY *CHECKED* IT--JUST *MINUTES* AGO!

THEN YOU CHECKED IT *WRONG!!*

LOOK AT THOSE *DIALS,* MAN!! THERE CAN'T BE ANY *DOUBT!!*

IF I HADN'T COME IN WHEN I *DID*--TO COMPENSATE FOR THE *SEEPAGE*--THERE'S NO TELLING *WHAT* MIGHT HAVE HAPPENED!!

SKLAAK!

I NEVER EXPECTED SUCH *CARELESSNESS* --IN A MAN OF YOUR REPUTATION, DOCTOR!!

MEANWHILE, TOO NERVOUS, TOO TENSE TO REMAIN AT THE BAXTER BUILDING WHILE THE VITAL *PREPARATIONS* ARE BEING MADE, THE BROODING *THING* WALKS AIM-LESSLY THRU THE CANYONS OF THE GREAT, SPRAWLING CITY--

THE ONLY THING I *REGRET*-- IN CASE THE EXPERIMENT *WORKS*--IT'LL MEAN THE FF WON'T *NEED* ME ANY MORE!!

WITHOUT MY *POWER*--I'LL JUST BE ANOTHER GUY NAMED BEN!

REED *KNOWS* HE'LL LOSE HIS *STRONGEST* PARD--BUT HE'S *STILL* TRYIN' TO HELP ME!

THAT EGGHEAD'S THE GREATEST *PAL* A GUY EVER *HAD!*

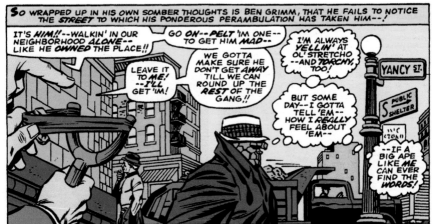

SO WRAPPED UP IN HIS OWN SOMBER THOUGHTS IS BEN GRIMM, THAT HE FAILS TO NOTICE THE *STREET* TO WHICH HIS PONDEROUS PERAMBULATION HAS TAKEN HIM--!

IT'S *HIM!!*--WALKIN' IN OUR NEIGHBORHOOD *ALONE*-- LIKE HE *OWNED* THE PLACE!!

GO *ON*-- PELT 'IM ONE-- TO GET HIM *MAD*--

LEAVE IT TO *ME!* --I'LL GET 'IM!

WE GOTTA MAKE SURE HE DON'T GET *AWAY* TILL WE CAN ROUND UP THE *REST* OF THE GANG!!

I'M ALWAYS *YELLIN'* AT OL' *STRETCHO* --AND *TORCHY,* TOO!

BUT SOME DAY-- I GOTTA TELL 'EM-- HOW I *REALLY* FEEL ABOUT 'EM--

YANCY ST.

PUBLIC SHELTER

--IF A BIG APE LIKE *ME* CAN EVER FIND THE *WORDS!*

SOMEHOW-- BEIN' WITH *THEM*-- I NEVER FELT SO MUCH LIKE--THE *MONSTER*-- I KNOW I REALLY *AM*--!

FTHAPP!

AND *ALICIA*--! ALL THESE YEARS-- SHE HELPED TO KEEP ME FROM-- DROPPIN' OUT--!

I DON'T *GET* IT! HE'S PICKIN' IT UP SLOW 'N EASY--LIKE NOTHIN' *HAPPENED!!*

ALICIA! THE SWEETEST KID WHO EVER LIVED!

IF WE CAN'T GET 'IM *MAD* AT US ANY MORE--THE *YANCY STREET GANG* MIGHT AS WELL GO OUTTA *BUSINESS!*

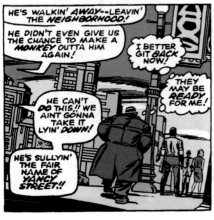

HE'S WALKIN' *AWAY*--LEAVIN' THE *NEIGHBORHOOD!*

HE DIDN'T EVEN GIVE US THE CHANCE TO MAKE A *MONKEY* OUTTA HIM AGAIN!

I BETTER GIT *BACK* NOW!

THEY MAY BE *READY* FOR ME!

HE CAN'T *DO* THIS!! WE AINT GONNA TAKE IT LYIN' DOWN!

HE'S SULLYIN' THE FAIR NAME OF *YANCY STREET!!*

AND, AS THE FRUSTRATED *YANCY STREETERS* GIVE VENT TO THEIR DISAPPOINTMENT...

FROM NOW ON, I'LL *DOUBLE-CHECK* EVERY STEP WE TAKE, DOCTOR!

SUIT YOURSELF-- RICHARDS--IF YOU FEEL IT'S *NECESSARY!*

[65]

THERE'S SOMETHING *ABOUT* SANTINI--THAT MAKES ME *MISTRUST* HIM!

I KNOW THAT *ANYONE* CAN MAKE A MISTAKE, SANTINI, BUT REMEMBER-- A HUMAN *LIFE* IS INVOLVED HERE--THE LIFE OF MY *BEST FRIEND!*

BUT, I CAN'T SAY ANYTHING TO *REED*--A WOMAN'S *INTUITION* IS HARDLY CONCRETE *EVIDENCE!*

I NEED NO FURTHER REMINDERS!

THE EXPERIMENT WILL *SUCCEED*-- EXACTLY AS I *PLANNED* IT!

I WAS *CARELESS* BEFORE--BUT LUCKILY, HE IS TOO *ANXIOUS* TO HELP THE *THING* FOR HIM TO CALL A *HALT* NOW!

AND SOON-- IT WILL BE *TOO LATE*-- FOR *ANY* OF THEM!

THEN, SUDDENLY--

RRKK!

IS EVERYTHING ALL *SET?? *IS SANTINI *READY* FER ME??

YOU'RE JUST IN *TIME!* THEY'VE BEEN *WAITING* FOR YOUR RETURN!

BEN!!

HEY! WHAT AM I DOIN' WITH A BLASTED *DOOR* IN MY-- -:UH OH!:-

I GUESS--I DID IT *AGAIN* --HUH?

DON'T WORRY ABOUT IT, OLD FRIEND!

THERE'S A *JOB* TO BE DONE!!

WELL?? LET'S *GIT STARTED!!*

I CAN'T WAIT TO LOOK IN THE *MIRROR*, 'N SEE *ROCK HUDSON* GRINNIN' BACK AT ME!

SUE--YOU'LL HAVE TO *LEAVE*, DEAR! THE RADIATION COULD BE *DANGEROUS!*

LET'S *GO*, SANTINI!

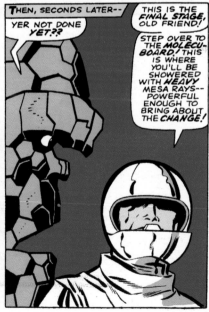

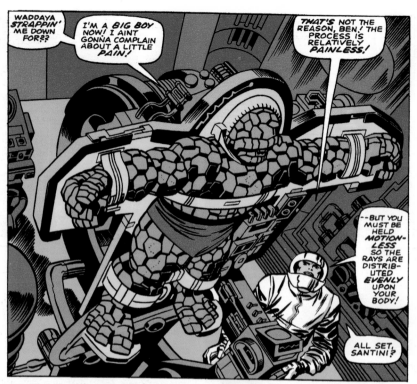

WAZZO!

IT'S *OVER!* NOW THERE'S *NOTHING MORE* THAT WE CAN DO!

IT'S *OVER,* HUH? THEN HOW COME I DIDN'T *CHANGE?* I'M STILL THE *SAME--!!*

I'VE NEVER SEEN THAT *EXPRESSION* ON BEN BEFORE!! SHEER *SAVAGERY* --AN AIR OF COMPLETE *MERCILESSNESS--* TOTAL *HATRED--!!*

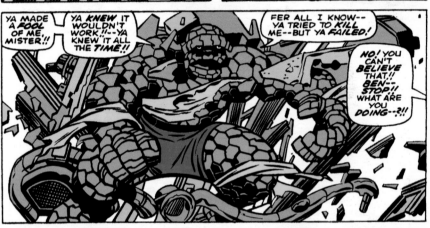

YA MADE A *FOOL* OF ME, MISTER!!

YA *KNEW* IT WOULDN'T *WORK!!--YA KNEW* IT ALL THE *TIME!!*

FER ALL I KNOW-- YA TRIED TO *KILL* ME--BUT YA *FAILED!*

NO! YOU CAN'T *BELIEVE* THAT!! BEN-- *STOP!!* WHAT ARE YOU *DOING--?!!*

I'M GONNA MAKE *SURE--* THAT YA'LL NEVER *LAUGH* AT ME-- AGAIN--!!

IT--IT'S *CLEAR* TO ME NOW!! YOU *DID* CHANGE!!

BUT--IT WASN'T --A *PHYSICAL* CHANGE!

SOMETHING WENT *WRONG!!* YOUR *BODY'S* THE *SAME--* BUT--YOUR *MIND* WAS AFFECTED--!!

AND NOW--HE'S COMING TO *KILL* YOU--!

JUST AS I *PLANNED!!* THE *THING* WILL ACCOMPLISH MY MISSION--HE WILL *DESTROY* THE FANTASTIC FOUR!

NEXT: --BY BEN BETRAYED!

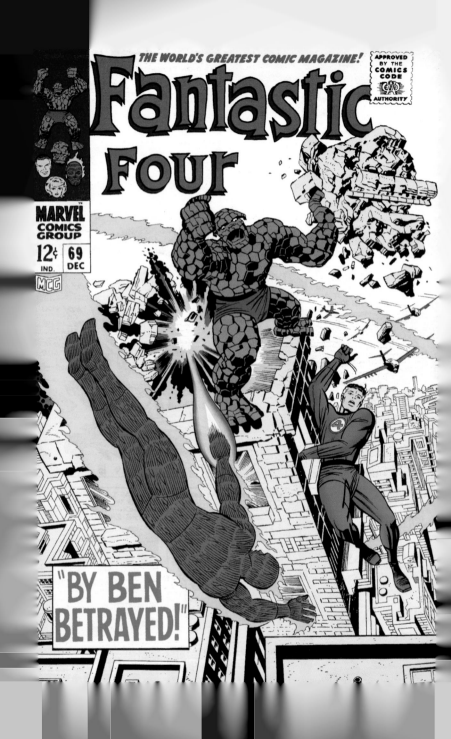

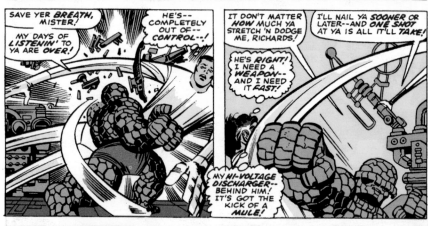

AT THAT MOMENT, *JOHNNY STORM* AND *CRYSTAL* RETURN TO THE BAXTER BUILDING, ONLY TO *HEAR*--

LISTEN! THE SOUND OF REED'S PORTABLE *DISCHARGER!* SOME-THING'S *WRONG!*

STAY BACK HERE, HONEY! I'D BETTER GO AND CHECK IT *OUT!*

BUT WHY CAN'T I GO *WITH* YOU?

NOT TILL I KNOW MORE *ABOUT* IT!

SECONDS LATER, JUST AS JOHNNY ENTERS THE LAB CORRIDOR--

THAT BOLT ALMOST *HIT* ME!

WHATEVER'S GOING *ON* IN THERE, I'M SURE OF *ONE* THING--IT'S FOR *REAL!*

ZAP!

FLAME ON!

THERE'S THE *DISCHARGER*-- RIGHT *AHEAD* OF ME!

CAN'T YET SEE WHO'S *HOLDING* IT FROM HERE--

BUT IT DOESN'T *MATTER!* ONE *FIRE BLAST* WILL TAKE *CARE* OF IT!

TZISSZ!

THE *TORCH!* HE *BLEW* IT UP!

BEN! IT WAS *YOU!!*--BUT, I DON'T *GET* IT!

WHY WERE YOU *FIRING* REED'S DISCHARGER??!

YA DON'T THINK THAT CORNY WALL OF *FLAME* IS GONNA STOP *ME* FER LONG!

I'LL WRITE'CHA A *BOOK!*

AND, ON THE *OTHER* SIDE OF THE NOW FLICKER- ING WALL OF *FLAME*--

WHAT ARE YOU *WAITING* FOR??

SURELY THAT LITTLE BIT OF DYING *FIRE* CAN'T STOP YOU!

WHAT'S THE *RUSH*, SANTINI? I CAN *GIT* 'EM ANY TIME I *WANNA*!

LET 'EM KNOCK THEMSELVES *OUT*--WONDERIN' WHEN I'LL TEAR *INTA* THEM!

YOU *FOOL!* TIME IS ON *THEIR* SIDE! RICHARDS HAS ALL HIS *EQUIPMENT* TO WORK WITH! YOU MUSTN'T LET HIM CONSTRUCT A NEW *WEAPON!*

YEAH! I NEVER *THOUGHT* OF THAT!

OKAY, RICHARDS-- PLAYTIME'S *OVER!* THIS IS *IT*, RAT!

THAT'S *IT!* THEY'RE JUST *AHEAD* OF YOU!

FINISH RICHARDS *FIRST*--AND THEN THE *OTHERS!*

AS FOR *ME*, I'VE JUST MADE THE GREATEST *FIND* OF ALL!

THE RAMPAGING *FOOL* JUST BROKE DOWN THE DOOR TO THEIR *FILE ROOM!*

EVERYTHING HAS HAPPENED JUST AS I *PREDICTED* IT WOULD!

NOT ONLY WILL I SUCCEED IN FINALLY *WIPING OUT* THE ACCURSED FANTASTIC FOUR--

BUT ALL OF RICHARDS' GREATEST *SECRETS* AND *FORMULAE* WILL BE *MINE!*

NEVER HAS ANYONE WON SO *GREAT*--SO TRULY *MONUMENTAL* A VICTORY!!

EVERYTHING I'VE EVER DREAMED OF ACCOMPLISHING--IS *HERE*-- IN THESE PRICELESS *PAPERS!*

AND NOW, THE TIME FOR *SUBTERFUGE* AND DISGUISE IS *ENDED!*

ONE BLAST OF MY SPECIAL *DISSOLVEX* GAS WILL OBLITERATE ALL MY PLASTIC *MAKE-UP*--AS WELL AS MY HASTILY-GROWN *MOUSTACHE*--

NEVER *AGAIN* WILL MEN CALL ME THE *MAD THINKER!*

FROM THIS MOMENT ON, I WILL BE *IMMORTALIZED* AS THE *ALL-POWERFUL THINKER*--

THE ONLY GENIUS ABLE TO COMPLETELY *WIPE OUT* THE FANTASTIC FOUR!

TO THOSE OF YOU WHO HAD ALREADY *GUESSED* THAT THE BOGUS SANTINI IS REALLY THE *MAD THINKER*, OUR SINCEREST *CONGRATULATIONS!* TO ALL OTHERS, DON'T REPROACH YOUR-SELVES--EVEN HONEST IRVING WAS TAKEN BY SURPRISE! AND NOW, BACK TO THE *TINTINNABULATIN'* TUMULT...

I *CAN'T* GO, MY DARLING! I I CAN'T LEAVE YOU TO FACE BEN *ALONE*--!

YOU *MUST*, SUE! I CAN'T LET YOU PLACE YOURSELF IN JEOPARDY --LEAST OF ALL *NOW!*

AS SOON AS I GET 'EM TO THE *PRECINCT HOUSE*, I'LL BE *BACK*, REED!

YOU'VE GOTTA *HANG ON* TILL THEN-- NO MATTER *WHAT!*

ARE YOU *SURE* THIS IS FOR THE *BEST* JOHNNY?

JOHNNY WILL TAKE BOTH YOU AND CRYSTAL TO *SAFETY!*

LET'S GO, SIS!! EVERY SECOND COUNTS!

IT'S *REED'S ORDERS*--AND THAT'S GOOD ENOUGH FOR ME, CRYS!

THEY'RE SAFE-- AT LAST!

NOW I CAN FACE THE *THING*--WITH NO *DISTRACTIONS*-- NO *INTERFERENCE!*

BE *CAREFUL*, REED! BE CAREFUL-- MY *DEAREST*--!

SHOOO

KRASH!

BEN!

[77]

BUT THE SUDDEN *JOLT* IS TOO MUCH FOR *MR. FANTASTIC* WHO IS SO PRECARIOUSLY BALANCED AT THE LIP OF THE LEDGE--

I MANAGED TO BREAK HIS *FALL*--BUT--

CAN'T HOLD *ON!* I'M-- GOING *OVER*--!

HE SLOWED ME DOWN *ENUFF* TO LET ME CATCH ONTO ONE'A THESE *GIRDERS!*

SO NOW I GOT ME A PERFECT *SPOT* TO WATCH RICHARDS WHEN HE FINALLY *HITS!*

BLAST IT!! I FORGOT!

HE CAN *FLATTEN OUT* THAT CRUMMY *BODY* OF HIS SO'S HE CAN *GLIDE* ALONG THE AIR CURRENTS!

BUT THAT AINT *SAVIN'* HIM FROM *ME!*

SKRUNCH

MOVE IT, YOU CREEPS!

THE *THING'S* GONNA TAKE A *RIDE* FER HIMSELF!

THERE AINT *NO* PLACE HE CAN FLOAT TO THAT I CAN'T *REACH* BEFORE HE GITS AWAY!

BUT, WHAT OF THE SINISTER SUPER-FIEND WHO *STARTED* IT ALL--??

SO FAR, EVERYTHING IS PROGRESSING ENTIRELY ACCORDING TO *PLAN!*

MY *COMPUTERS* PREDICTED I WOULD SNAP *PICTURES* OF RICHARDS' MOST TREASURED SECRETS AT THIS VERY *MOMENT...*

HIS *SOLAR-ENERGY ACTIVATOR* ALONE IS WORTH ALL THAT I'VE RISKED!

AND RICHARDS' *COMPUTERS!* I NEVER DREAMED THAT *ANYONE* COULD CREATE VARIATIONS WHICH EVEN *I* HAD NEVER THOUGHT OF!

MY *OWN* COMPUTERS *PREDICTED* THAT I'D FIND THE MOST AWESOME DISCOVERY OF *ALL* AT THIS SPLIT-SECOND!

THIS MUST BE IT-- BEHIND THE STEEL *DOOR!*

BUT--WHY SO *STRONG* A DOOR?? WHY THE WORD *DANGER??*

NEGATIVE ZONE COMPLEX

DANGER!

WHAT DOES IT *MEAN??* WHAT --HAVE I-- STUMBLED *INTO--??!*

AND THE *SAME* GOES FOR THE DESPERATE MISTER FANTASTIC--

THE *AIR CURRENTS* ARE FAR TOO *STRONG*--CAN'T CHANGE *DIRECTION* IN TIME!

I'M BEING BLOWN-- HELPLESSLY--STRAIGHT TOWARDS THAT SHARP-POINTED *SPIRE--!*

BUT, BEFORE THE FANTASTIC ADVENTURER CAN *STRIKE* THE DEADLY STEEPLE...

A BLAZING *FIREBALL*-- MELTED IT INTO *NOTHING-NESS!*

LOOKS LIKE I MADE IT *BACK* JUST IN *TIME!*

YOU *KNOW* IT, BROTHER-IN-LAW!

COVER ME, JOHNNY-- AS I HEAD FOR THE *RIVER!*

LOOKS LIKE HE'S TRYIN' FOR A LANDIN' IN THE *WATER!*

WELL, IT AINT GONNA BE AS EASY AS HE *THINKS*--NOT IF *I* CAN HELP IT!

HE'S STARTIN' TO GLIDE *LOWER!*

AN' THAT MAKES IT JUST *PERFECT* FER ME!

ALL I GOTTA *DO* IS REACH THAT OLD, EMPTY, TEN-STORY *TOWER* JUST AHEAD!

THUMP!

IT'S GONNA BE TORN DOWN *ANYWAY*-- TA MAKE ROOM FER THE NEW *EXPRESS-WAY*--

AN' SINCE I'M A *REAL,* BIG-HEARTED, PUBLIC-SPIRITED *CITIZEN*--

NO PARKING
SAT---
DAY---

I'LL JUST KIND'A *SPEED UP* THE JOB A LITTLE!

FTOOM!

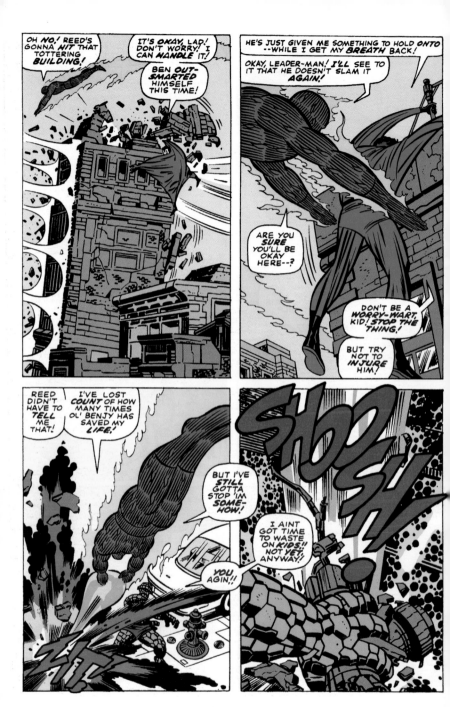

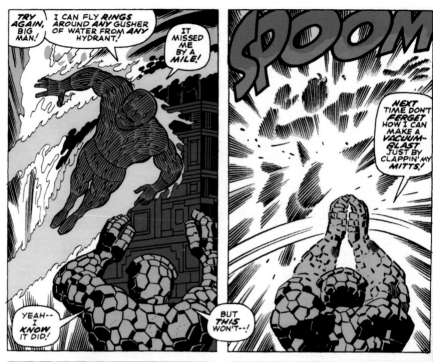

WE'RE DOING EVERYTHING WE *CAN,* MRS. RICHARDS!

EVERY AVAILABLE MAN IS BEING RUSHED TO THE SCENE RIGHT *NOW!*

ARE YOU SURE YOU'VE HEARD *NOTHING??* NO WORD AT *ALL?*

HERE'S THE *SCRAMBLE ORDER* TO ZONE D! WE'RE TAKING NO *CHANCES!*

MOVE IT, MAN!

THIS IS *IT,* YOU GUYS!

THEY'VE JUST BEEN SIGHTED IN THE *MURRAY HILL* SECTION!

WE'RE GONNA THROW EVERYTHING WE'VE *GOT* INTO THE AREA!

IF THERE'S *ANY* WAY TO HELP REED RICHARDS, WE'LL *FIND* IT, LADY!

IF ONLY--WE COULD BE SURE--THE *THING* WON'T BE HARMED, AS WELL!

LOOK, MRS. RICHARDS.!! YOU CAN'T HAVE IT *BOTH* WAYS!

THAT *NOISE* OVERHEAD!! THE SOUND OF *ENGINES--* JET PLANES--!

THAT ORANGE-SKINNED *POWER-HOUSE* ISN'T GONNA BE STOPPED BY A PAT ON THE *WRIST!*

I *TOLD* YOU WE WERE PULLIN' ALL THE STOPS! WE CAN'T LET SOMEONE AS STRONG AS THE *THING* RUN RIOT IN THIS TOWN!

JETS!! THEY MUST BE COMIN' FER *ME!*

NUTS! IT'LL TAKE A LOT MORE'N *THAT* TO KEEP ME FROM GITTIN' MY HANDS ON *RICHARDS!!*

'N AFTER I *DO--* I DON'T GIVE A HANG *WHAT* HAPPENS!

THEN, ONCE THE SHIP IS SAFELY OUT OF RANGE--

QUICK! CONTACT THE *JETS!* HAVE THEM *RETURN TO BASE!!* THE *THING* MUST *NOT* BE HARMED!

I'LL ASSUME *ALL* RESPONSIBILITY!

THE ORDER'S BEEN *GIVEN*, SIR!

YOU WERE *WONDERFUL*, SUE! YOU *SAVED* ME --WITHOUT HARMING BEN!

BUT--HOW LONG CAN WE *PROTECT* HIM, DARLING?? WHAT WILL *BECOME* OF HIM?

MAY HEAVEN HELP US-- I... DON'T KNOW!!

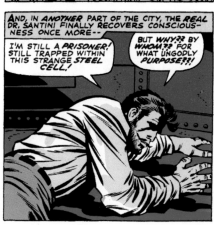

AND, IN *ANOTHER* PART OF THE CITY, THE *REAL* DR. SANTINI FINALLY RECOVERS CONSCIOUSNESS ONCE MORE--

I'M STILL A *PRISONER!* STILL TRAPPED WITHIN THIS STRANGE *STEEL CELL!*

BUT *WHY??* BY *WHOM??* FOR WHAT UNGODLY *PURPOSE??!*

OVER *THERE*-- A *FIGURE*-- BEHIND THAT PLEXIGLASS *WINDOW!!*

IF I CAN JUST *SIGNAL* HIM--ATTRACT HIS *ATTENTION*--!! PERHAPS HE CAN *HELP* ME--!!

IT'S *NO USE!!* HE DOESN'T *MOVE!!* HE SEEMS AS *LIFELESS* AS A *STATUE!*

IN FACT--HIS *HEAD*-- WHAT I CAN *SEE* OF IT--ISN'T *HUMAN!!* HE'S--AN ANDROID OF SOME SORT--!!

BUT WHO *CONTROLS* HIM?? WHO'S *BEHIND* IT *ALL??*

AND, IN ANSWER TO SANTINI'S DESPERATE QUESTION, WE RETURN TO THE *MAD THINKER*, AS HE BEHOLDS AN AWESOME SIGHT--

SO!! RICHARDS HAS FOUND THE ENTRANCE TO *SUB-SPACE*--

HE'S DISCOVERED THE DREADED *NEGATIVE ZONE* ITSELF..!!

THE *NEGATIVE ZONE!!* THE *ONE* THING MY *COMPUTERS* COULD NOT PREDICT--THE ONE *EXTRA* FACTOR!!

BUT, EVERYTHING *ELSE* HAS GONE ACCORDING TO MY *COMPUTATIONS!*

THERE WAS A *99.68%* POSSIBILITY THAT THE *THING* HAS FINISHED *REED RICHARDS* BY NOW!

AND YET--I MUST NOT *DISCOUNT* THE *.32%* POSSIBILITY OF AN *UPSET!*

IF RICHARDS *SURVIVED,* HE IS CERTAIN TO GUESS MY *REAL* IDENTITY!

IN WHICH CASE, IT WON'T TAKE HIM LONG TO FIND WHERE I'VE IMPRISONED *SANTINI!*

THAT MEANS I'VE GOT TO *RETURN* AS SOON AS POSSIBLE--AND DISPOSE OF THE LIVING *EVIDENCE!*

THE *NEGATIVE ZONE* WILL HAVE TO *WAIT*-- --UNTIL I'VE MADE CERTAIN TO COVER ALL MY *TRACKS!*

AND NOW, BACK TO OUR HARRASSED HEROES--

WE LEARNED YOU HAD BROUGHT THE *TORCH* HERE!

CAN WE *SEE* HIM?? IS HE *ALL RIGHT?*

SURE, RICHARDS! WE MANAGED TO REACH HIM IN PLENTY OF TIME!

THE BOY IS *FINE!*

HE'S *WAITING* FOR YOU-- RIGHT *INSIDE*--!

JOHNNY! THANK HEAVENS YOU'RE NOT *HURT!* WE WERE SO *WORRIED!*

NUTS! I WAS *SOME* GREAT HELP!

YOU'D HAVE DONE BETTER *WITHOUT* ME!

NO, DON'T SAY THAT! HOW COULD *YOU* KNOW THAT BEN WAS OUT TO *DESTROY* US??

I *STILL* CAN HARDLY BELIEVE IT!

WHERE DO WE GO FROM *HERE,* REED?

I'VE BEEN WRACKING MY BRAIN-- AND I THINK I'VE FOUND THE *KEY!*

SANTINI IS RESPONSIBLE FOR ALL THIS! BUT, THE *REAL* SANTINI WOULD HAVE NO *MOTIVE!* HE'S BEYOND *REPROACH!*

OF *COURSE!* IT'S THE ONLY *ANSWER!* WE WERE DECEIVED BY AN *IMPOSTOR!!*

--BY SOMEONE OUT TO *DESTROY* US!

BUT *WHO?*

I THINK I HAVE THE *ANSWER* TO THAT ONE--!

HIS PREOCCUPATION WITH *COMPUTERS*--HIS DETAILED, SEEMINGLY FOOL-PROOF *PLAN*-- HIS KNOWLEDGE OF SCIENTIFIC *PROGRAMMING* --HIS COMPLEX, YET BRILLIANTLY EXECUTED *MOVES*--

IT ALL ADDS UP TO *ONE* DIABOLIC- ALLY DANGEROUS FIGURE--

CAPTAIN! IF I GIVE YOU HIS LAST KNOWN LIST OF *HIDEOUTS*, WILL YOU ORDER AN IMMEDIATE CITY- WIDE *SEARCH* FOR--

--THE *MAD THINKER?!!*

I'LL LEAD THE SEARCH *MYSELF,* RICHARDS!

GOOD! THERE'S NOT A *MINUTE* TO LOSE!

SANTINI'S LIFE IS IN GREATER *PERIL* EACH SECOND THAT THE THINKER REMAINS *FREE!*

YOU *HEARD* THE MAN, SERGEANT! *ALERT* ALL *UNITS!!*

CANCEL ALL LEAVES! I WANT EVERY VEHICLE ON THE STREET THAT'S ABLE TO *ROLL*--AND I WANT 'EM *NOW!*

YES *SIR,* CAPTAIN!

WE'RE ON OUR WAY!

WHILE, ATOP THE DOOMED, STILL- SMOLDERING BUILDING--

THERE'S COPS 'N FIREMEN ALL *OVER* THE PLACE!

BUT THEY AINT GONNA BE ABLE TO STOP ME!!

NOTHIN'S GONNA STOP ME TILL I PUT THE *KIBOSH* ON RICHARDS--FER THE *LAST* TIME!

I CAN MAKE IT TO THE ROOF *BELOW* BY HANGIN' ONTO THIS SAGGIN' *DRAINPIPE!*

THE *SMOKE'LL* GIMME ENOUGH *COVER* TO DO WHAT I GOTTA DO BEFORE THEY *FIND* ME!

'N IF ANYONE *DOES* CATCH UP WITH ME-- THAT'S SURE GONNA BE *HIS* HARD LUCK!!

A COAT 'N *HAT!* JUST WHAT I *NEED!*

KEEP THE *CROWD* BACK, MARTY!

WHAT D'YA FIGURE MADE HIM TURN *BAD* THAT WAY, BILL?

AS LONG AS THE *THING'S* ON THE LOOSE--NOBODY'S GONNA BE SAFE *ANYWHERE!*

I DUNNO! BUT HE BETTER BE *FOUND*--AND FINISHED OFF --BUT *FAST!*

WHEN SOMEONE LIKE *HIM* TURNS KILLER--YOU CAN'T TAKE ANY *CHANCES!*

HE'S GOTTA BE *STOPPED*--FOR GOOD--LIKE YOU'D STOP A MAD *DOG!*

RICHARDS TURNED *EVERYONE* AGAINST ME! BUT IT AINT GONNA *HELP* 'IM!

I KNOW ALL HIS *TRICKS!*--ALL HIS *SECRETS!*

--'N I GOT ALL THE MUSCLE I NEED-- TO *FINISH OFF* THE FF--FOREVER!

NEXT:
ONE DOWN
TWO TO GO!

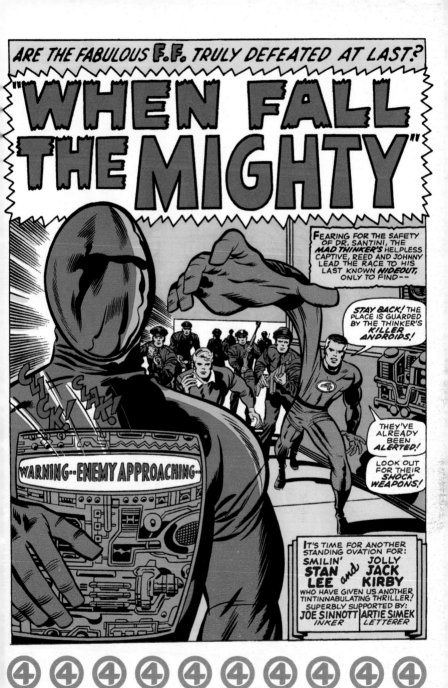

THIS FINISHES THE *LAST* OF THEM!

BUT KEEP YOUR *EYES* PEELED! THE *THINKER* USUALLY HAS ONE *SUPER-POWERED* ANDROID THAT HE KEEPS IN RESERVE!

NOW WE'VE GOTTA FIND *SANTINI!*

THERE'S NO SIGN OF ONE *HERE!*

FOLLOW RICHARDS, MEN!

HE KNOWS THE *THINKER'S* STRATEGY BETTER THAN *ANYONE!*

TORCH! FLAME ON AHEAD!

BUT *CAREFUL,* LAD!

ALL CLEAR SO FAR!

NO *SIGN* OF HIM *YET!*

SLOW DOWN, JOHNNY!

DON'T GET *OVER-CONFIDENT!*

DON'T EVER *FORGET*-- HE'S MOST *DANGEROUS* WHEN HE TAKES YOU BY *SURPRISE!*

YOUR WORDS ARE *TRUER* THAN YOU *THINK,* RICHARDS!

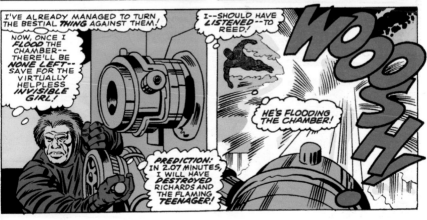

I'VE ALREADY MANAGED TO TURN THE BESTIAL *THING* AGAINST THEM!

NOW, ONCE I *FLOOD* THE CHAMBER-- THERE'LL BE *NONE LEFT*-- SAVE FOR THE VIRTUALLY HELPLESS *INVISIBLE GIRL!*

PREDICTION: IN 2.07 MINUTES, I WILL HAVE *DESTROYED* RICHARDS AND THE FLAMING *TEENAGER!*

I--SHOULD HAVE *LISTENED*--TO REED!

HE'S FLOODING THE CHAMBER!

WOOOSH!!

BUT, IF YOU THINK A LITTLE *FLOOD* IS ALL OUR HEROES HAVE TO WORRY ABOUT, *FORGET IT!* LOOK WHO *ELSE* IS HERE--/

DAILY BUGLE

THING RUNS AMOK! CITY-WIDE DRAGNET!

RICHARDS AINT IN THE *BAXTER* BUILDING!

BUT HE CAN'T HIDE FROM ME *FOREVER!*

I'LL FIND 'IM *SOONER* OR LATER-- AND THE SAME GOES FOR THAT PUNK *TORCH*, ALSO!

SO EVERYONE'S *LOOKIN'* FOR ME, HUH?

WELL, IT'LL BE *TOO BAD* FER THE ONE WHO'S DUMB ENUFF TO *FIND* ME!

EVERYONE'S WALKIN' AROUND LOOKIN' *SCARED!*

--LIKE THEY EXPECT ME TO POP UP OUTTA THE *WOODWORK*, OR SOMETHIN'!

WELL, MEBBE THEY *OUGHTTA* BE SCARED!

EVER SINCE RICHARDS TRIED SANTINI'S *MACHINE* ON ME-- 'N IT DIDN'T *WORK*-- I GOT NO USE FOR *NOBODY!**

BATTLE ATOP CITY H...

THING RUNS AMOK! CITY-WIDE DRAGNET!

LET'S GET HOME *RIGHT* AWAY!

IF THE THING REALLY *HAS* TURNED BAD-- *NO ONE* WILL BE SAFE!

*THAT'S WHAT *STARTED* THE WHOLE THING, REMEMBER? THE *TINKER* TAMPERED WITH THE EXPERIMENT OF *REED* AND *SANTINI*, CAUSING THE MACHINE TO AFFECT BEN'S BRAIN! --SOUL-OF-SINCERITY STAN.

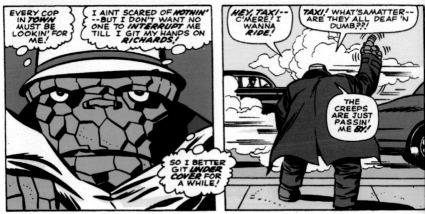

EVERY COP IN *TOWN* MUST BE LOOKIN' FOR ME!

I AINT SCARED OF *NOTHIN'* --BUT I DON'T WANT NO ONE TO *INTERRUPT* ME TILL I GIT MY HANDS ON *RICHARDS!*

SO I BETTER GIT *UNDER COVER* FOR A WHILE!

HEY, TAXI!-- C'MERE! I WANNA *RIDE!*

TAXI! WHAT'SAMATTER-- ARE THEY ALL DEAF 'N DUMB,??!

THE CREEPS ARE JUST PASSIN' ME *BY!*

WHILE, BACK AT *FF HQ*, AT THAT VERY MOMENT, THERE IS *ANOTHER* WHO PONDERS THE SAME QUESTION--

IF BEN EVER *CATCHES* REED AND JOHNNY--WHAT *CHANCE* WILL THEY HAVE?

NO, SUE! YOU MUSTN'T *SAY* THAT! YOU MUSTN'T EVEN LET YOURSELF *CONSIDER* SUCH A THING!

ESPECIALLY AT A TIME LIKE *THIS*-- WHEN YOU SHOULD BE *UNTROUBLED*-- UNWORRIED!

BUT--JUST BECAUSE-- I'M GOING TO HAVE A *BABY*-- MUST I FORSAKE MY *HUSBAND*-- AND MY *BROTHER??*

THEY MAY *NEED* ME NOW--MORE THAN EVER BEFORE!

YOUR *BABY* WILL NEED YOU *TOO,* SUE DEAR--!

YOU *KNOW* THAT'S THE WAY *REED* AND *JOHNNY* WOULD WANT IT!

*N*OW THAT WE'VE DEMONSTRATED HOW *HARD* WE TRY NOT TO LOSE TRACK OF OUR SEEMINGLY *COUNTLESS* CHARACTERS, LET'S *RETURN* TO THE FLAMING FIREBRAND WHO HAS WON CRYSTAL'S HEART--

SO FAR I'VE MANAGED TO STAY *ABOVE* THE FLOODWAVE--

BUT, IF IT GETS ANY *HIGHER*-- ENDSVILLE!

OKAY THEN, TORCHY-- THERE'S ONLY *ONE* THING TO *DO*--!

DON'T *LET* IT GET ANY HIGHER!

I SHOULD BE ABLE TO *DRAIN* MOST OF IT OFF--

BY BURNING A DEEP *PIT* RIGHT IN THE PATH OF THE TORRENT!

THANK *HEAVENS!* HE'S STILL *ALIVE!*

HIS *FLAMING BODY* WAS ABLE TO *ABSORB* THE IMPACT--

BUT THE SUDDEN *SHOCK* KNOCKED HIM OUT!

OKAY, THINKER --WHEREVER YOU *ARE*--THE GLOVES ARE *OFF!*

NOW *I'M* COMING AFTER YOU --*MYSELF!*

PREDICTION: RICHARDS *WILL* REACH ME IN EXACTLY 43.9 SECONDS!

WHICH WILL BE *TIME ENOUGH* FOR ME TO *DISPOSE* OF SANTINI-- BEFORE WE COME *FACE-TO-FACE!*

COME *OUT,* DR. *SANTINI!* YOUR FINAL *FATE* AWAITS YOU!

TO *ME* YOU WERE NO MORE THAN A *MACHINE*--ONE WHICH EXISTED MERELY TO *SERVE* ME!

AND, WHEN A MACHINE *OUT-LIVES* ITS PURPOSE-- THERE IS NOTHING TO DO BUT *DESTROY* IT!

SKRAKK

YOU--WOULD *MURDER* ME-- IN COLD BLOOD?

MURDER IS SUCH AN *UNPLEASANT* WORD!

LET US SAY, INSTEAD, THAT I SHALL *DISPOSE* OF SOME EMBARRASSING *EVIDENCE!*

SORRY, FRANTIC ONE--WE MUST INTERRUPT AGAIN--BUT VERY BRIEFLY--AS A SUBWAY WORK CREW MAKES A STARTLING DISCOVERY--

GIT THAT *LIGHT* OUTTA MY EYES-- OR *ELSE*--!

HEY! IT'S THE *THING!*

I DUNNO ABOUT *YOU*--BUT FOR ME IT'S *QUITTIN'* TIME!

TAKE *OFF,* YA CREEPS!

NUTS! NOW THEY'LL SPREAD THE *ALARM!*

QUICK! THERE'S AN *EXIT* JUST AHEAD!

BUT THAT *DELAY* WAS ALL I *NEEDED*--

TO GET THE *WHIP HAND* ONCE AGAIN!

MY COMPUTERS *PREDICTED* A HAND-TO-HAND STRUGGLE BETWEEN US./

BUT I AM *NOT WORRIED!*

DESPITE YOUR ACCURSED *FLEXIBLE LIMBS*-- AND YOUR SUPERIOR *SKILL*--YOU ARE BATTERED AND BRUISED--YOU ARE *WEARY*-- ON THE VERGE OF *EXHAUSTION!*

THEREFORE, MY *FINAL PREDICTION*--

TOTAL *VICTORY* FOR THE *THINKER* IN EXACTLY ONE MINUTE AND FOURTEEN SECONDS!

ALL RIGHT, MURDERER-- YOU *HAD* YOUR SAY--!

BUT *AGAIN* YOU'VE MADE ONE *FATAL MISTAKE!*

YOU DIDN'T TAKE INTO ACCOUNT A MAN'S *FIGHTING SPIRIT!*

THE SPIRIT THAT MAKES A MAN *GO ON*--

EVEN THOUGH HIS *BODY* CAN TAKE *NO MORE*--!

THE SPIRIT THAT MAKES A MAN WILLING TO *DIE* FOR WHAT HE *BELIEVES* IN--

THE SPIRIT THAT *NO* COMPUTER --*NO* ELECTRONIC THINKING MACHINE--

WILL *EVER* BE ABLE TO MEASURE-- OR TO *PREDICT!*

AT THAT VERY MOMENT, *OUTSIDE* THE GRIM, FATEFUL CHAMBER--

ARE YOU SURE YOU'RE *STRONG* ENOUGH NOW, KID?

I'VE *GOT* TO BE! *ANYTHING* COULD BE HAPPENING TO MY *PARTNER* IN THERE RIGHT NOW!

IF I CAN JUST *MELT DOWN* THE CONTROL DEVICES WHICH MAINTAIN THE ELECTRO-BARRIER--! *THERE!* IT'S *WORKING!*

YOU *DID* IT! YOU *DISSOLVED* THE BARRIER!

LET'S GO, MEN!

REED! WHAT *HAPPENED* IN HERE??

ARE YOU *OKAY?*

I'M-- *ALL* RIGHT--!

HE'S THE *ONE*--WHO MADE POOR *BEN*--TURN *BAD!*

THEN YOU WERE *RIGHT* ALL ALONG!

THE MAD THINKER IMPERSONATED DR. SANTINI!

WHAT *ABOUT* SANTINI--?

HE JUST NEEDS *REST!* HE FOUGHT--WITH GALLANTRY!

I GUESS EVERYTHING'LL BE *OKAY* NOW, EH?

OKAY?! HAVE YOU *FORGOTTEN*--??

THE *THING* IS STILL AT LARGE--HIS *BRAIN* TWISTED BY THE *THINKER'S* EVIL MANIPULATIONS--!

BUT WE'LL *FIND* HIM--AND *EXPLAIN* EVERYTHING, WON'T WE, REED?

THAT'S JUST *IT!* WE *CAN'T* EXPLAIN! HE'S *TOO FAR GONE!* HE'S OUT TO *DESTROY* US!

AND--HE HAS THE *POWER*--TO DO IT!

YES, THE *POWER*--AND THE *STRENGTH*--AND THE UNBRIDLED *HATRED*, AS WELL--!

JUST ANOTHER FEW BLOCKS 'N I'LL BE *THERE!*

NO ONE'S GONNA STOP ME *NOW!*

SUB
DOW
42

I SHOULD'A REALIZED *LONG AGO* THAT RICHARDS IS MY *ENEMY!*

THAT'S WHY I GOTTA *SMASH* THE FANTASTIC FOUR!

I GOTTA *WIPE* 'EM OUT-- FOREVER!

IT'S THE ONLY WAY TO *PAY 'EM BACK*-- FER WHAT THEY *DID* TA ME!!

WHILE, BACK AT THE EX-SCENE OF BATTLE--

WHAT DO WE DO *NEXT*, REED?

HOW ARE WE GONNA FIND-- *POOR BEN?*

I'VE A HUNCH THAT *HE'LL* BE FINDING *US*, JOHNNY-- AS SOON AS HE *CAN!*

THEN SHOULDN'T WE BE *PREPARING* SOMETHING?

I'M 'WAY *AHEAD* OF YOU, LAD!

IF I CAN MANAGE TO *POSITION* BEN AT JUST THE RIGHT SPOT IN MY LAB--!

BUT, BEFORE THE GRIMLY DETERMINED *REED RICHARDS* CAN UTTER ANOTHER WORD--

THOOM!

LOOK OUT!

AWRIGHT, RICHARDS-- THIS IS *IT!*

HE'S *HERE!*

BEN!

THAT'S *IT*, RICHARDS-- *HANG ON!*

THE LONGER IT *TAKES*, THE MORE I'M GONNA *ENJOY* CLOBBERIN' YA!

MY STRENGTH --ALMOST *GONE!*

WHAT HAPPENS *NEXT*-- WHEN HE ATTACKS *AGAIN!*

BUT, STILL *ANOTHER* DEADLY PROBLEM IS A'BORNING FOR THE DESPERATE FF--

I DON'T *GET* IT!

THE *MAD THINKER* HAS BEEN *BEATEN*-- HE'S TRAPPED IN A *CELL*--

LET 'IM GRIN!

THERE'S NOTHING HE CAN *DO* --WHILE HE'S LOCKED IN *THERE!*

AND STILL HE'S GRINNIN' LIKE HE'S GOT AN *ACE* UP HIS SLEEVE!

MAN! IF THEY ONLY *KNEW!*

IT IS NOW TIME FOR ME TO TURN *AWAY*--AS THOUGH I'M LOOKING OUT OF THE WINDOW-- LOST IN *THOUGHT!*

BUT--THE THOUGHTS I AM THINKING HAVE ONLY *ONE* PRIME PURPOSE--

THE *DESTRUCTION* OF THE FANTASTIC FOUR!

LUCKILY, THEY DID NOT TAKE MY *WRIST-WATCH* FROM ME--

FOR, HOW COULD THEY SUSPECT THAT IT'S FAR *MORE* THAN A SIMPLE TIME-PIECE?

PREDICTION: WITHIN 6.09 SECONDS IT WILL SIGNAL MY MOST POWERFUL *ANDROID* TO PERFORM ITS PRE-PROGRAMMED TASK--!

EXACTLY 6.09 SECONDS LATER, AN INDESTRUCTIBLE, 12-FOOT TALL FIGURE SEEMS TO COME *ALIVE*--

SMASHING THRU THE SOLID-STEEL DOOR OF ITS SECRET CRYPT WITH ONE EFFORTLESS MOTION--!

SLOWLY, INEXORABLY, THE EMOTIONLESS CREATURE'S *MAGNETIC SHOES* BRING HIM UP THE SIDE OF THE *BAXTER BUILDING*... TOWARDS THE FATEFUL *35th FLOOR*--!

THO OM! THOOM!

THE SOUNDPROOF FLOOR WHERE THE GRIM, DEADLY *BATTLE* NEARS ITS ULTIMATE CONCLUSION--

NOW, WHILE BEN'S *BACK* IS TOWARDS ME--

THIS IS MY *CHANCE* --AT *LAST*!

THE *MENTA-WAVE UNIT* IS AIMED *RIGHT* AT HIM--!

CLAK!

FZZZT!

--ARRHHHH!

REED! YOU--YOU *DID* IT! HE'S *COLLAPSING!*

BUT--HE--HE'S *NOT BREATHING*--ANY MORE--!

YOU'VE *KILLED*--HIM!!!

THEN, AT THAT VERY INSTANT--

SOMETHING *TERRIBLE* IS HAPPENING IN THERE--I JUST *KNOW* IT!

I'M ALMOST AFRAID--TO OPEN THE *DOOR!*

THAT *NOISE*--INSIDE--

--LIKE SOMETHING SMASHING DOWN THE WALL!

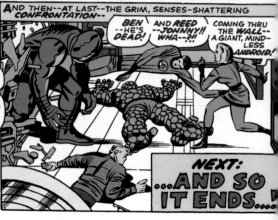

AND THEN--AT LAST--THE GRIM, SENSES-SHATTERING *CONFRONTATION*--

BEN --HE'S *DEAD!*

AND *REED* --*JOHNNY!!* WHA--?!!

COMING THRU THE *WALL*--A GIANT, MIND-LESS *ANDROID!*

NEXT: ...AND SO IT ENDS...!

IT *WORKED!* BUT...

IT GENERATED *TOO MUCH* POWER!! IT'S *CRACKLING* THROUGHOUT THE ENTIRE *LAB...!*

IT'S *HITTING BEN...* LIKE A *SUDDEN LIGHTNING BLAST!!*

IT'S AFFECTED *ALL* OF US... EVEN *JOHNNY!*

BUT IT WAS A STROKE OF *LUCK!!* IT'S *REVIVING* THEM ALL!!

THE *ANDROID* ABSORBED THE *MAIN* FORCE...BUT, IT DIDN'T *HURT* HIM!

REED, DARLING--- *WAKE UP!! HURRY!!*

SUE! YOU *SAVED* US... BY GAINING US *TIME!*

BUT NOW... *TAKE COVER!* THE ANDROID *SENSES* HE MUST *DESTROY* HIS INVISIBLE ENEMY!

HIS HEAD IS *CONVERTING* TO *RADAR-SCAN FUNCTION...* TO PICK UP YOUR IMAGE!!

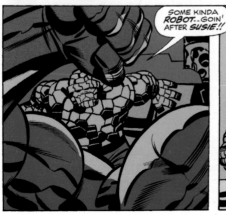

BUT, SUE'S SUDDEN *ELATION* IS DESTINED TO BE TRAGICALLY *SHORT-LIVED*...FOR, A SPLIT-SECOND LATER, THE MIGHTY ANDROID FIRES THE *POWER JETS*, LOCATED IN ITS BACK, DIRECTLY INTO A STARTLED BEN GRIMM--!

SHOOP!

BEN'S STRENGTH *SAVED* HIM... BUT, HE'S *HURT*... WEAKENED!!

AND THE ANDROID IS ABOUT TO ATTACK *AGAIN!!*

MY *INVISIBLE FORCE FIELD!!*

IT'S GOT TO *CUSHION* THE BLOW...GIVE BEN TIME TO *RECOVER* HIMSELF!!

IT *WORKED!* HE'S SNAPPING *OUT* OF IT AGAIN!

SO YER LOOKIN' FER SOME *ACTION*, HUH??

OKAY, CHARLIE-- IN CASE NOBODY *TOLD* YA---

IT'S CLOBBERIN' TIME!!

6.

WHILE, ON THE THIRTY-FIFTH FLOOR---

OKAY, JUNIOR...YA CAN KNOCK OFF THE *FIREWORKS!*

I AIN'T NO *TALENT SCOUT* FOR THE ED SULLIVAN SHOW!

SORRY, BEN! I JUST COULDN'T TAKE ANY *CHANCES!*

YOU PROBABLY DON'T *REMEMBER*... BUT THE *MAD THINKER* FOUND SOME WAY TO TURN YOU *AGAINST* US, AND---

HEY!!

NOW WHAT?!!

BEHIND YOU, BEN *!!* COMING IN FROM OUTSIDE *!! LOOK..!!*

IT'S THE CRUMMY *ROBOT!!* THE ONE I BELTED CLEAN THROUGH THE *WALL!*

WHAT'S HE TRYIN' TA *DO*...MAKE ME FEEL *INSECURE??*

IT'S NO JOKE, BEN!

HE'S PROBABLY *INDESTRUCTIBLE!*

WATCH IT!! HE'S ATTACKING!

GLAD YA *TOLD* ME, BRIGHT EYES!!

HOW CAN BEN *STOP* HIM??

THOOM!

HE DOESN'T EVEN FEEL MY *EXPLOSIVE FLAME-BLASTS!*

11.

[125]

THERE'S STILL *ONE* THING I CAN DO...

I'LL *INTENSIFY* MY FLAME... MAKE IT HOT ENOUGH TO *MELT* HIS CIRCUITS!!

I'M BETTIN' HE *UNDERSTANDS* YA!

LOOKA THE WAY HE'S *TURNIN'* AROUND!

BUT THEN, BEFORE THE THING CAN MAKE ANOTHER MOVE...

GAS!!... SHOOTIN' OUTTA HIS *FINGERS!*

GETTIN' IN MY *LUNGS* ...CHOKIN' ME... CAN'T... *BREATHE*..!

SHOOSH!

BEN *COLLAPSED!!*

...AND THE *ANDROID*... HE'S CAUSING HIS *BODY TEMPERATURE* TO *DROP*...

BELOW THE *FREEZING POINT!*

NOW HE'S HURLING BLASTS OF *COLD* AT ME...

JUST AS HE INUNDATED BEN WITH THE *GAS!*

HOW DO YOU *BEAT* SOMEONE LIKE THAT??

HE CAN DO ALMOST *ANYTHING!*

EVEN THOUGH I CAN DODGE THE *BLASTS*...

THE *COLD WAVE* IS FILLING THE ENTIRE *LAB!!*

I CAN'T MAKE MY FLAME *HOT* ENOUGH TO WITHSTAND IT!

NOT WITHOUT *SCORCHING* REED, BEN AND SUE!!

12

THEN, WITHIN A MATTER OF SECONDS, THE *INEVITABLE* OCCURS...

I'M...*TRAPPED* AGAINST---THE WALL---

ENCLOSED IN...AN *ICE-CRYSTAL* ENVELOPE!!

MY FLAMES-- CAN'T ESCAPE!! *PRESSURE* IS INCREASING--!!

AND, AS THE PRESSURE MOUNTS BEYOND THE POINT OF *ENDURANCE*...

SPLANNG!

THEN, WHEN THE SMOKE HAS CLEARED...

REED! THAT *EXPLOSION!!* WHAT *WAS* IT..??

I DON'T *KNOW*, DEAR! BUT, IT CAN ONLY MEAN NEW *DANGER!*

I'VE GOT TO GO *BACK!*

13.

AT THAT MOMENT, THE LOVELY *CRYSTAL* REAPPEARS...

SUE, I HAVE THE *TONIC* YOU SENT ME FOR, AND... *SUE*!!

WHAT'S *WRONG*?? WHAT *HAPPENED*??

ANSWER ME... SOMEBODY!!

HERE, CRYSTAL!! IN *HERE*..!!

DON'T... ENTER THE LAB...NO MATTER *WHAT*!!

SUE!! WHAT IS IT?? *TELL* ME!!

WHERE ARE *JOHNNY*... AND THE *OTHERS*??

IT'S *QUIET* IN THERE NOW! THAT MEANS ---IT'S *OVER*!!

BUT... I'M *AFRAID*!! ---AFRAID TO EVEN *HOPE*..!!

NO *NEED* TO BE! LOOK... *BEHIND* YOU..!!

IT'S *ALL RIGHT*, DARLING!!

WE *WON*!!

BUT, *JOHNNY*!! WHERE IS *JOHNNY*..?

HE'S INSIDE! *GO* TO HIM, CRYSTAL! I'VE GOT TO *LOOK* AFTER *SUE*! SHE'S BEEN THROUGH ---SO *MUCH*!

JOHNNY!! WHERE *ARE* YOU?

IT'S *ME*-- CRYSTAL!

I'M *HERE*, JOHNNY!! I'M *HERE*!!

18

PERHAPS WE SHOULD ALL TAKE A NICE *VACATION!*

...SOMEPLACE LIKE *FLORIDA*... OR *BERMUDA!*

YEAH! CAN'TCHA JUST *SEE* ME IN A BEACH CHAIR AT THE *FONTAINEBLEU?!*

I'D *CLEAR OUT* THE BLASTED BEACH FASTER THAN A HOWLIN' *HURRICANE!*

WE *CAN'T* LEAVE NOW, CRYS! NOT WITH REED AND SUE GONE!

IT'S MORE IMPORTANT THAN *EVER* FOR US TO STAY AND CARRY ON!

BUT....YOU HAVE YOUR *OWN* LIVES TO LEAD, TOO!

I *KNOW* IT, HONEY! DON'T *TEMPT* ME, GIRL!

NUTS!! NUTHIN' BUT *TALK, TALK, TALK!*

WHAT'S A CLOBBERIN' KID LIKE *ME* DOIN' IN A NOWHERE PLACE LIKE *THIS?*

WHY DON'T YOU CALL *ALICIA,* BEN?

DON'T *RUSH* ME, KID... DON'T *RUSH* ME!

DIDJA EVER STOP TO THINK WHAT *HAPPENS* WHEN I CALL HER?

I'M ALWAYS SCARED SHE'LL SAY SHE'S AWREDDY *GOT* A DATE!!

BUT THAT'S A CHANCE *ANY* FELLA TAKES...!

BUT ANYONE *ELSE* AIN'T... THE *THING!*

WHAT'S GONNA HAPPEN TO ME WHEN SHE *FINDS* HERSELF ANOTHER JOE?

CAN YA PICTURE *ME* COMPETIN' WITH SOME JOKER WHO AIN'T A REFUGEE FROM A MIDNIGHT *MON-STER* SHOW?!!

HOLD IT, BEN! WHAT'S *THIS*...?

JOHNNY! *LOOK*..!

YOU MUST ALL *FORGET* YOUR PETTY PROBLEMS!

BY MEANS OF A *DIMENSION WARP,* I HAVE COME TO *WARN* YOU ...OF TERRIBLE *DANGER!!*

SOME-ONE'S POPPIN' UP... OUTTA *NO-WHERE!!*

2.

SURELY YOU REMEMBER... THE *WATCHER!*

THOUGH I AM PLEDGED NEVER TO MEDDLE IN THE AFFAIRS OF OTHER PLANETS...THERE IS SOMETHING YOU *MUST KNOW!*

THE SUPREMELY-POWERFUL *SILVER SURFER* IS ABOUT TO ATTACK *ALL OF MANKIND!!*

THE *SURFER!!*

BUT...HE'S PRACTICALLY... *INVINCIBLE!!*

BUCKLE YER *SEAT BELTS,* KIDDIES!

HERE WE GO *AGAIN!*

BUT YOU *CAN'T* BATTLE SO *MIGHTY* A FOE... WHEN YOU HAVE LOST *HALF* OF YOUR TEAM!

AND, SPEAKING OF THE OTHER HALF OF THE WORLD-FAMED *FANTASTIC FOUR*...LET'S VISIT A CALIFORNIA-BOUND TRANSCONTINENTAL EXPRESS...

HOW WILL THE *OTHERS* GET ALONG *WITHOUT US,* DARLING?

I *TOLD* YOU NOT EVEN TO *THINK* OF THAT, SUE!

ALL THAT MATTERS NOW IS *YOUR* WELFARE... AND THAT OF---THE *BABY!*

DON'T FORGET, HONEY... *BEN GRIMM* IS ONE OF THE MOST *POWERFUL* OF ALL LIVING BEINGS!

AND THE *HUMAN TORCH* ISN'T EXACTLY LACKING IN SUPER-POWER *HIMSELF!*

BUT, SO LONG AS WE'RE AWAITING THE BABY, IT'S *YOU* WHO ARE THE MOST *VULNERABLE!*

WE'VE GOT TO BE *CERTAIN* THAT NO DEADLY *ARCH-ENEMY* TRIES TO *STRIKE* AT US... BY MENACING MY *WIFE!*

NOW LET'S FORGET ABOUT SUCH SORDID THINGS...AND START ENJOYING THE *SCENERY!*

3.

NO NEED TO TELL HER THAT I'M AS CONCERNED ABOUT BEN AND JOHNNY AS *SHE* IS!

DESPITE THEIR *STRENGTH*, WE'VE ALWAYS FOUGHT AS A *TEAM*....THE *FOUR* OF US!

BUT *NOW*....IF ANY *NEW* MENACE SHOULD ARISE....!

I *KNOW* HE'S ONLY TRYING TO KEEP MY *SPIRITS* UP....!

JOHNNY IS *YOUNG*, DEAREST....WITH HIS WHOLE LIFE *AHEAD* OF HIM---

WHILE BEN, THAT SOFT-HEARTED CURMUDGEON, IS VIRTUALLY *INDESTRUCTIBLE!*

IT'S *YOU* I MUST THINK OF NOW....*YOU* WHO MUST BE *PROTECTED!*

BUT, I MUSTN'T *UPSET* HIM...

HE'S SACRIFICED SO *MUCH* FOR ALL OF US ALREADY!

YOU... AND THE *BABY* THAT WILL SOON BE *OURS!*

OKAY, FRANTIC ONES... SOAP OPERA TIME'S *OVER!* NOW, BATTEN DOWN THE HATCHES....'CAUSE *WE'RE OFF*....!

WHEREVER I TRAVEL, O'ER THE FACE OF THIS BATTLE-SCARRED PLANET...

I FIND EVER-INCREASING EXAMPLES OF MAN'S *INHUMANITY* TO HIS FELLOW MAN!

HERE, ON THE FAIREST OF ALL WORLDS---HERE, WHERE MORTALS COULD CREATE A LIVING *UTOPIA*---

THE VERY *AIR* I BREATHE SEEMS TAINTED WITH THE ARID STENCH OF *BIGOTRY, HATRED, GREED,* AND *OPPRESSION!*

BUT, IF MEN REFUSE TO TURN AWAY FROM WANTON, UN-THINKING *SAVAGERY*...

--THEN SHALL THE *SILVER SURFER* SHOW THEM THE *FATE* THAT MUST BE *THEIRS!*

4

THE ONLY WAY TO MAKE THEM *CEASE* THEIR CONSTANT WARRING IS TO PROVIDE FOR THEM A *COMMON FOE!*

LET THEM *UNITE*... TO BATTLE *ME*... THE *ULTIMATE* ENEMY!

IT CAN CAUSE *VEGETATION* TO GROW MADLY... WILDLY...

SNARLING VILLAGES, TOWNS, AND CITIES!

NO NATION-- NO CONTINENT-- SHALL BE *SPARED* THE ATTACK OF THE *SILVER SURFER!*

FOR, MY *COSMIC POWER* CAN ACCOMPLISH *ANYTHING!!*

I CAN CAUSE THE *SEAS* THEM-SELVES TO RISE IN MOUNTAINOUS *FURY*---

TILL NONE WHO LIVE WILL *DARE* TO SAIL THEM!!

NOT EVEN THE ETERNAL *PYRAMIDS* WILL ESCAPE MY *DE-GRAVITY* THRUST!!

5

THOUGH HE MANAGED TO BURN HIS WAY *THRU...*

IT *WEAKENED* HIM---AS I KNEW IT *MUST!*

AND NOW...I SHALL QUICKLY *COUNTERATTACK!...*

...EMPLOYING HIS *OWN* MIGHTY WEAPON *AGAINST* HIM!

THEN, MOVING AT A SPEED WHICH THE FLAMING YOUTH CANNOT EVEN *HOPE* TO MATCH, THE *SILVER SURFER* MAKES AN INCREDIBLE TRAP OF COSMIC *TORCHES* ATOP THE SURROUNDING SKYSCRAPERS...!

HE'S...HEMMING ME *IN...*

WITH TOWERS OF...*COSMIC FORCE!!*

THEY'RE GROWING IN INTENSITY---CLOSING *IN* ON ME!

THE ENERGY IS *BLINDING... DAZZLING...*

I...DON'T KNOW ...WHICH WAY TO *TURN...!!*

BUT, SUDDENLY...

OKAY, CHARLIE...

NOW LET'S SEE HOW YA DO AGAINST SOMEONE YER OWN *SIZE!!*

AND, BEFORE THE STARTLED *SURFER* CAN MAKE ANOTHER MOVE---

I GOTTA PUT 'IM OUTTA ACTION *FAST*...

BEFORE HE CAN TOSS ONE OF THEM CRUMMY *BOLTS* AT ME!

HOLD STILL, BLAST YA!!

A FELLA CAN GIT *AIR SICK* THE WAY YER WIGGLIN' AROUND UP HERE!

BUT, BEFORE THE ORANGE-SKINNED HUMAN *POWERHOUSE* CAN LAND A TELLING BLOW, HIS STAR-SPAWNED OPPONENT JABS HIM WITH A PAIR OF TWIN, STINGING *ENERGY WAVES*...!

THE SILVER SURFER IS *NOT* SO EASILY *BESTED!*

NOR DOES *YOUR* BESTIAL STRENGTH IMPRESS ONE WHO HAS BEEN HERALD TO--- *GALACTUS!*

FOR, I *TOO* POSSESS *MIGHT* BEYOND MEASURE!

≡UNHHH!≡

10.

[145]

NO MATTER *HOW* POWERFUL ONE MAY BE...

SOMEWHERE... SOMEHOW... THERE IS ALWAYS *SOMEONE* WHO IS HIS *MASTER!*

AND NOW... I HAVE *TIRED* OF THIS GAME!!

AT THAT MOMENT, ON THE SPEEDING TRANSCONTINENTAL EXPRESS...

BILL! UP AHEAD!!!

WHAT IN THE NAME OF HEAVEN IS *THAT?*

IT LOOKS LIKE A... A...

NO! IT *CAN'T* BE! IT ISN'T *POSSIBLE!*

IT *IS!* IT'S SOME KINDA *MAN*... STANDING ON THE *TRACKS*... RIGHT *AHEAD* OF US!

BUT... LOOK AT THE *SIZE* OF HIM!!

WE'RE GONNA *HIT* 'IM! WE'LL NEVER *STOP* IN TIME!!

NO!! HE JUST... *WAVED* HIS HAND... AND *LOOK*...!

WE *STOPPED*... WITHOUT EVEN A *LURCH*...

LIKE FLOATING ON A *CLOUD!!*

DO NOT FEAR! I MEAN *NO HARM!*

THERE ARE TWO *PASSENGERS* UPON YOUR MULTI-WHEELED CONVEYANCE...

I WISH TO *SPEAK* TO THEM... AT *ONCE!*

12

SUE! He means US!

WHAT COULD HAVE *HAPPENED*... IMPORTANT ENOUGH--- TO BRING THE *WATCHER* HERE ??

MY EXPLANATION SHALL BE *BRIEF*...

FOR, EVERY *MOMENT* IS VITAL!

THE *SILVER SURFER*...UNMINDFUL OF THE DREAD *CONSEQUENCES* ... NOW RUNS *AMOK* AMONGST MANKIND!

THOUGH *I* AM *FORBIDDEN* TO ENTER THE FRAY---

SAY NO MORE!!

I KNOW WHAT MUST BE DONE!

NO, REED! NOT--- *YOU*!!

CAN'T YOU *SEE?* I *MUST* GO! IT WILL TAKE ALL OUR *POWER.*

THEN *I'LL* GO, TOO!

NO!! I FORBID IT!

THE DECISION IS *MADE*!!

SO SHALL IT *STAND!*

HE'S--- *TRANSPORTING* ME---TO THE SCENE---! *WAIT* FOR ME---MY DARLING---!

REED! I'LL WAIT--- *FOREVER*!!

BUT WHAT...CAN HE *DO*---AGAINST THE ALL-POWERFUL *SILVER SURFER*??

ALL-POWERFUL? THERE IS ONLY *ONE* WHO DESERVES THAT NAME!

AND *HIS* ONLY WEAPON... IS *LOVE!*

BUT, *LOVE* IS THE LAST THING ON ANYONE'S MIND AT THIS PARTICULAR MOMENT! AND, IF YOU THINK WE'RE KIDDING...

WHAT'S THAT?? ORDERS FROM THE PENTAGON?!

WE'RE TO USE THE *SONIC SHARK** AGAINST THE *SURFER*?

YOU *BET!* SHE'S *FULLY-OPERATIONAL* NOW!

CLEAR THE AREA... ON THE DOUBLE!

* SONIC SHARK: AN EXPERIMENTAL MISSILE WHICH HARNESSES AND UNLEASHES THE POWER OF *COSMIC ENERGY!!* ...*PSEUDO-SCIENTIFIC* STAN.

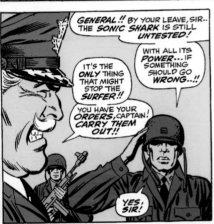

GENERAL!! BY YOUR LEAVE, SIR.. THE *SONIC SHARK* IS STILL *UNTESTED!*

WITH ALL ITS *POWER*... IF SOMETHING SHOULD GO *WRONG*...!

IT'S THE *ONLY* THING THAT MIGHT STOP THE *SURFER!!*

YOU HAVE YOUR *ORDERS*, CAPTAIN! *CARRY THEM OUT!!*

YES, SIR!

BEGIN THE COUNT-DOWN!!

NO MATTER *WHERE* THE SURFER IS...

OUR BIRD'LL *FIND HIM*... AND BRING 'IM *DOWN!*

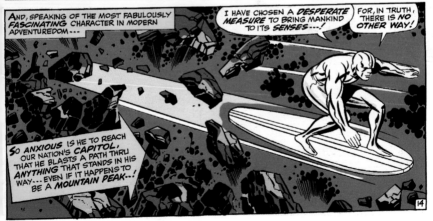

AND, SPEAKING OF THE MOST FABULOUSLY *FASCINATING* CHARACTER IN MODERN ADVENTUREDOM---

I HAVE CHOSEN A *DESPERATE MEASURE* TO BRING MANKIND TO ITS *SENSES*---!

FOR, IN TRUTH, THERE IS *NO OTHER WAY!*

SO ANXIOUS IS HE TO REACH OUR NATION'S *CAPITOL,* THAT HE BLASTS A PATH THRU *ANYTHING* THAT STANDS IN HIS WAY... EVEN IF IT HAPPENS TO BE A *MOUNTAIN PEAK*--!

14

BUT, WE SEEM TO HAVE *FORGOTTEN* SOMETHING! OH, YES... THAT'S RIGHT... *REED RICHARDS*...

HE *DID* IT!

THE WATCHER *TELEPORTED* ME BACK TO THE ROOF OF A MIDTOWN BUILDING!!

BUT, WHO IS--*OH!* JOHNNY!

WHAT *IS* IT, BOY? WHAT *HAPPENED*??

OHHH... MY *HEAD!*

IT WAS THE *SILVER SURFER!!* HE *PULVERIZED* ME WITH SOME *COSMIC BOLTS!*

THAT'S NOT IMPORTANT, LAD!

WHAT I HAVE TO *KNOW* IS... *WHERE'S THE SURFER NOW??*

BUT... *REED!* WAIT A MINUTE! HOW'D YOU GET *BACK* HERE?

I'M NOT *SURE!* I *LOST* HIM!

BUT---WHAT HAPPENED TO *BEN*??

HE WAS RIGHT *WITH* ME!

THERE'S ONLY *ONE* WAY TO FIND OUT---

WE'VE GOT TO FIND THE *SURFER!*

LUCKILY, WE'RE ONLY A FEW BLOCKS AWAY FROM OUR *BAXTER BUILDING* HEADQUARTERS!

SO *FLAME ON*, PARTNER!

T-H-W-I-P!

...AND *AWAAAAAAY* WE GO!!

15

HE MUST BE IN ONE BIG *HURRY!*

HE'S FIXIN' TA *GRAB* ME WITH THAT NUTTY *SKY HOOK..!*

HANG ON, BEN! WE'VE NO TIME TO SLOW DOWN!

YEAH! YEAH! I KINDA *NOTICED!*

DIDJA FIND THE *SURF..* HEY!

HOLD IT! WHERE'S THE *TORCH??*

HE FLEW ON *AHEAD...* TO *SAVE* TIME!

NOW *SIT TIGHT...* I'M SHIFTING TO *ROCKET SPEED!*

BUT, EVEN AS REED RICHARDS *SPEAKS...*

THE DEADLY SONIC SHARK IS *LAUNCHED!!*

AND, AS IT UNERRINGLY HOMES IN ON ITS SPEEDING, STREAKING, SKY-RIDING VICTIM---

THE *SURFER'S* JUST AHEAD *!!*

I'VE GOTTA DO SOMETHING... *NOW!!*

THE SURFER'S *LANDING!*

BUT... HE LOOKS *HURT!*

FLAME OFF, JOHNNY! STAY *BACK!*

WAIT FOR *US!*

YOU NEED HAVE--NO FURTHER *FEAR*...OF THE *SILVER SURFER!*

ONCE AGAIN...I HAVE *UNDERESTIMATED*...THE AWESOME CREATIONS OF *MAN!!*

BEFORE THE WEAPON *EXPLODED*...IT *WEAKENED* ME--

IT HAS...ALMOST TOTALLY *DRAINED* ME--OF MY *COSMIC POWER!*

THUS, I STAND BEFORE YOU... NO LONGER *INVINCIBLE*...

NO LONGER *MAD* ENOUGH TO FEEL THAT *ONE BEING ALONE* COULD BRING *SANITY* TO THE HUMAN RACE!

THEN, SOMEHOW, IT WAS ALL...*WORTHWHILE!*

YOU SURE GOTTA LEARN THINGS THE *HARD WAY!*

ONCE AGAIN, THE *SILVER SURFER* IS IN YOUR *DEBT!*

YOU OWE US *NOTHING!*

YOU SHALL NOT FIND ME *UNGRATEFUL!*

JUST REMEMBER--MANKIND IS *NOT* AS LOST...*NOT* AS HOPELESS... AS IT MAY *SEEM!*

TRULY, THERE IS A SPARK OF *DIVINITY* IN ALL WHO *LIVE,* AND *THINK*...AND *STRIVE!*

A SPARK THAT WILL ONE DAY *IGNITE*...

--AND *ILLUMINATE* THE UNIVERSE!!

≟SHEEESH!≟ BILLY GRAHAM'S GOT NOTHIN' ON *YOU!*

WELL, HE'S *GONE* AGAIN!

YOU JUST CAN'T *HOLD* A GENT LIKE THAT!

AND I'M KINDA *GLAD* OF IT!

HEY! WITHOUT HIS *COSMIC POWER,* HE'S LIKE ANY *JOE*...ON A FLYIN' SURFBOARD!

HE'LL NEVER BE --LIKE ANY *JOE!*

IN ALL THE UNIVERSE-- THERE'LL NEVER BE ANOTHER LIKE-- THE *SILVER SURFER!*

--EXCEPT FOR NEXT ISSUE'S SENSATIONAL GUESTS, **SPIDEY, THOR,** and **DAREDEVIL!**

20

WITH *DOOM* ABOUT TO STRIKE, I'M GLAD THERE WAS TIME TO GET *SUE* SAFELY OUT OF TOWN!

YOU WON'T HAVETA *WORRY* ABOUT THAT CREEP--

NOT IF HE GITS WITHIN *CLOBBERIN'* DISTANCE!

ANYWAY, HOW CAN YA BE *SURE* THAT OL' *HORNHEAD* IS REALLY *DOOM?*

I *SEE* HIM-- JUST AHEAD!

BECAUSE THE *REAL* DAREDEVIL CALLED TO *WARN* US!

BUT HOW D'YA KNOW IT *WUZ* THE REAL DD?

DON'T YOU REMEM- BER--?

WE CHECKED HIS *VOICE* AGAINST THE AUDIO RECORD ON ON OUR *VOCA-FILE!*

*A*ND, AS WE CONCLUDE OUR SNEAKY, SUB- LIMINAL *SUMMARY--*

IT'S HARD TO BELIEVE THAT *DOOM* IS REALLY *GONE!*

BUT, I *STILL* HAVE TO WARN THE *FF--*

THERE'S ALWAYS THE CHANCE HE MAY TRY THE SAME TRICK *AGAIN--*

BUT, ONCE I REVEAL HIS SECRET OF *BODY TRANSFERRAL* TO RICHARDS, HE'LL-- *WAIT!!*

IT CAN ONLY MEAN-- *ONE* THING--!

THAT SUDDEN *HEAT--* ABOVE ME!

ZASK!

THE *TORCH!* HE'S *ATTACKING!*

BUT *WHY?*

WHY USE HIS *FLAME* AGAINST *ME?!!*

2

HI, GOLDILOCKS! YOU'RE JUST THE THUNDER GOD I'VE BEEN *LOOKING* FOR!

SPIDER-MAN! WHAT BRINGS THEE HENCE?

I WAS *HOPING* YOU'D ASK!

THERE'S *TROUBLE* BREWING BETWEEN THE *FF* AND *DAREDEVIL*, AND--

STILL THY TONGUE! I'LL HEAR *NO MORE* OF IT!

THE POWER OF *THOR* IS NEEDED ELSE-WHERE!

WOW! - I NEVER THOUGHT *YOU'D* TURN CHICKEN!

IF THAT DOTH MEAN WHAT I *TAKE* IT TO MEAN--

THOU DAREST ACCUSE THE SON OF ODIN-- OF *COWARDICE??*

YOU FIGURE IT OUT, CURLY!

EVEN AS WE *TALK*, DAREDEVIL'S LIFE IS IN DANGER--FROM THE *FF!*

CAN'T WAIT FOR *SPIDER-MAN* ANY LONGER!

THE *BAXTER BUILDING* IS JUST AHEAD!

MY *RADAR SENSE!!* IT JUST *REACTED* TO SOMETHING! I'D BETTER---*UNN!!*-

TOO LATE! I'VE BEEN SNARED-- BY *RICHARDS* HIMSELF!

YA *GOT* 'IM, STRETCH!

BUT, WHAT HAPPENED TO *JOHNNY?*

THAT'S WHAT WE'LL SOON FIND OUT!

HOW DO I *CONVINCE* THEN I'M THE *REAL* DAREDEVIL ??

IF THEY THINK I'M *DR. DOOM* --THEY WON'T GIVE ME A *CHANCE!*

5

LEGGO OF HIM, MISTER!

IT DON'T TAKE *BRAINS* TO HANDLE A CRUMB *THAT!*

NO, BEN! WE'VE GOT TO FIND OUT WHAT HE DID TO THE *TORCH* FIRST!

BEN--*STOP!!* HOLD IT!

DON'T BE A *FOOL,* THING!

I'M NOT DR. *DOOM!*

OH *NO?!* THEN WHY-- *UNNNH!*

YER *NERVE BLAST* RAY!! YA USED IT-- AGAINST-- *ME?!!*

I *WARNED* YOU, BEN!

I HAD A *FEELING* IT WASN'T MY *KICK* THAT STOPPED HIM!

LOOK, RICHARDS-- USE YOUR *HEAD!*

OF *COURSE* YOU WOULD--

IF I *WERE* DOOM-- WOULD I COME *HERE?*

IF YOU DIDN'T KNOW THE *REAL* DAREDEVIL HAD ALREADY *WARNED* US!

BUT--GIVE ME A *CHANCE* --I'LL *PROVE* WHO I AM!

HOW?

HE'S *RIGHT!!* --NOW!!

WE *BOTH* KNOW DOOM HAD A *BODY TRANSFERRAL* RAY--

SO, HOW DO I *PROVE* HE HASN'T *USED* IT ON ME?

LET'S SIT DOWN AND *TALK* ABOUT IT--LIKE CIVILIZED MEN!

FORGET IT, MASKED MAN!

BETWEEN THE *TWO* OF US WE CAN FIGURE SOMETHING OUT!

IF YOU *ARE* DR. DOOM-- I WOULDN'T LET MY *GUARD* DOWN FOR A SECOND!

THEN-- WHAT DO YOU PLAN TO *DO*--

--*MURDER* ME--JUST ON *SUSPICION??*

6

THAT DON'T SOUND LIKE A BAD IDEA, FROM WHERE *I* SIT!

HOLD OFF, BEN! YOUR FULL STRENGTH *CAN'T* HAVE RETURNED TO YOU SO *SOON!*

NUTS!! HOW MUCH DO I *NEED* AGAINST THAT FOULBALL?

I KIND'A HATE TO MESS UP DAREDEVIL'S BODY--SINCE IT DON'T *BELONG* TO YA--

HAVE TO STRIKE *NOW*--WHILE HE'S PARTIALLY *STUNNED!*

--BUT I'LL *APOLOGIZE* WHEN I *SEE* 'IM!

-:*UNNNN!!*:- EVEN AFTER BEING BELTED WITH RICHARDS' *NERVE BLASTER*--

HE'S *STILL* A POWERHOUSE!

RATS!! I TRIPPED OVER STRETCHO'S MILE-LONG *LEG!!*

THE *DEMOLO-GUN*-- YOU'RE *FALLING* TOWARDS IT!

LOOK OUT, BEN!

LOOK OUT!

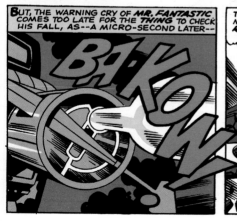

*B*UT, THE WARNING CRY OF *MR. FANTASTIC* COMES TOO LATE FOR THE *THING* TO CHECK HIS FALL, AS--A MICRO-SECOND LATER--

BA-KON

THE SHOCK MADE HIM *RELEASE* ME!

THIS IS MY CHANCE TO *ESCAPE*--

IF I CAN MANAGE TO *LIVE* LONG ENOUGH!

THE *DEMOLO-GUN!!*

SMASH IT, BEN--*SMASH* IT!

7

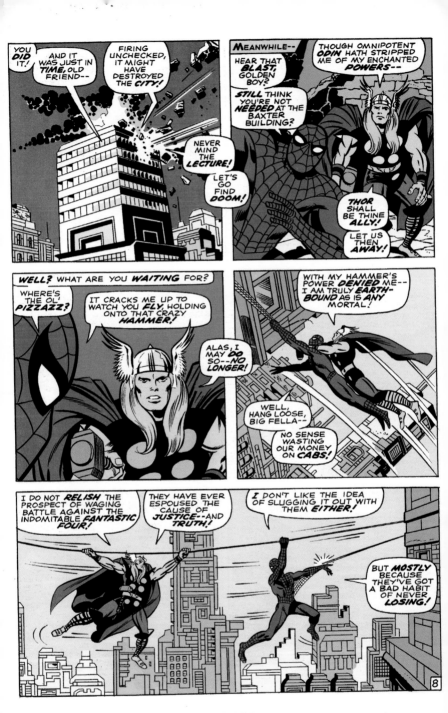

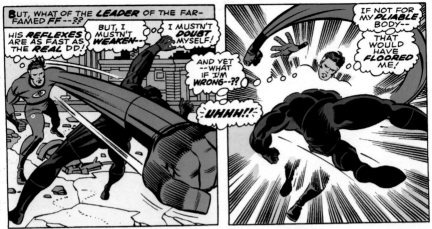

BUT, REACHING OUT FROM UNDER THE ENVELOPING BODY OF REED RICHARDS, DAREDEVIL'S UNCANNY *SENSES* DIRECT HIS HAND TO--

SOME SORT OF ELECTRIC *POWER ROD!*

I'VE GOT TO *SHOCK* HIM WITH IT--LONG ENOUGH TO BREAK *FREE!*

--UNHH.!--

HOW--COULD YOU SPOT THAT *ROD*-- WHEN I HAD YOU--TOTALLY *BLIND- FOLDED??*

THAT'S *MY* SECRET!

NOBODY CAN OPERATE SO WELL WITHOUT BEING ABLE TO *SEE*--

--UNLESS HE HAPPENS TO BE-- AN ELECTRONIC *ROBOT!*

--SUCH AS THE TYPE *DR. DOOM* EXCELS IN CREATING!

HE DOESN'T REALIZE MY *OTHER* SENSES MAKE UP FOR MY LIFELONG *BLINDNESS!*

NOW, DUE TO MY OWN *POWER,* HE'S *SURE* TO BELIEVE I'M ONE OF DOOM'S *ROBOTS!*

HE'S MAKING A *LASSO--* OF HIS *ARM!*

ALL RIGHT, MASKED MAN-- *JUMP!*

THANKS! JUST WHAT I *WANTED!*

15

AND, AT THAT MOMENT, *ANOTHER* MEMBER OF THE MULTI-POWERED *FF* IS ALSO DOING WHAT COMES NATURALLY--

WHAT'S KEEPIN' YA ON YER *FEET,* CURLEY?

WHEN I *BELT* A GUY, HE'S SUPPOSED TO *STAY* BELTED!

YOU TRYIN' TO GIMME A *COMPLEX,* OR SOMETHIN'?

O, MOST IMPERIAL *SIRE*-- THOUGH THOU HAST MADE ME *LESS* THAN GODLIKE--

STILL AM I TRULY *MORE* THAN MORTAL!

THOUGH I HAVE BEEN *FORSAKEN* BY THEE--

NEITHER MY *FAITH*-- NOR MY *TRUST* HAVE WAVERED!!

THUS, IN *THY* NAME--

BECAUSE I BE *FLESH OF THY FLESH*--*BLOOD OF THY BLOOD*--

THE *VICTORY* SHALL YET BE *MINE!*

SO SPEAKS *THOR!!*

I DON'T *GIT* IT! HOW CAN ANY BLASTED *ROBOT* MANAGE TO TALK AS CORNY AS *THAT*--?

YEWWPH!

16

THIS IS *BATTY,!!* EVEN THOUGH WE *KNOW* WE'RE SUPPOSED TA *FLATTEN* THE WHOLE BUNCH'A YA--

WE KEEP *PULLIN'* OUR PUNCHES--ON ACCOUNT'A YA LOOK LIKE THE *GOOD GUYS!*

WITLESS, CHURL! DOST THOU TAKE US FOR *KNAVES?*

THINK YOU WE BE *LESS* THAN WHAT WE *SEEM?*

HOW'S A GUY TO KNOW *WHAT* TO THINK--WITH YOU TALKIN' LIKE A REFUGEE FROM A ROAD-SHOW *HAMLET!*

I *CAN'T* MAKE MYSELF TEAR INTA HIM--I JUST *CAN'T!*

TO THINK THAT THE ONCE-PROUD *FANTASTIC FOUR* HAVE TURNED TO CRAVEN *SAVAGERY!*

NOW YA DID IT.! I AINT SURE I KNOW WHAT YA *SAID*--

--BUT IT SOUNDED TO ME LIKE YER *PUTTIN' DOWN* THE *FF*--

AND *NOBODY* DOES THAT WHILE *BASHFUL BENJAMIN'S* AROUND!!

17

THEN, EVEN AS THE *THING* STANDS IN MUTE MYSTIFICATION--

I THOUGHT *YOU* HAD MORE SENSE THAN THE *OTHERS*, RICHARDS!

I HOPED *YOU'D* LISTEN TO REASON--!

TRY ME, FELLA!

I'M STILL *WAIT-ING* FOR SOME *PROOF* FROM YOU!

BUT, I *TOLD*--

I DON'T KNOW *HOW* TO PROVE I'M *ME*!

SUPPOSE *YOU* HAD TO PROVE YOU WERE REALLY *YOU*--

HOW WOULD YOU *DO* IT?

IT'S A GOOD *ARGUMENT*, MISTER! YOU SHOULD HAVE BEEN A *LAWYER*!

BUT IT SO HAPPENS I *KNOW* WHO I AM!

YOU'RE THE ONE I'M WORRIED ABOUT!

NOW, *TALK!!* TELL ME WHERE THE *REAL* DR. DOOM IS, AND I'LL-- *WHA--??!* WHAT STOPPED MY BLOW FROM *LANDING??*

I *DID!*

THAT *VOICE!* IT CAN ONLY BE--!!

SUE! BUT--YOU SHOULDN'T *BE* HERE--!

I *HAD* TO COME, DARLING--TO SAVE YOU--FROM A *TERRIBLE MISTAKE!*

HE *IS* THE *REAL* DARE-DEVIL!

BUT--HOW CAN *YOU* KNOW?

19

IT WAS ON THE SIX P.M. *TV NEWS!* DOOM'S IN *LATVERIA*--HE WAS ADDRESSING A CONFERENCE OF MINISTERS! THEN, WHEN I LEARNED *SPIDER-MAN, THOR,* AND *DAREDEVIL* WERE SEEN AT THE *BAXTER BUILDING*--AND AN EXPLOSION WAS REPORTED-- I *COULDN'T* STAY AWAY!

I'M SURE GLAD YOU'RE A TV *FAN,* MRS. RICHARDS!

I GUESS THAT CLEARS THINGS UP, DD!

AND *THIS* TIME HE MEANS *DAREDEVIL*-- *NOT* DOC DOOM!

I FIGGERED IT WUZ YOU GUYS ALLA TIME!

NO BLAMED *ROBOTS* COULD FIGHT LIKE THAT!

WELL, AS *MAYOR LAGUARDIA* USED TO SAY-- WHEN I MAKE A MISTAKE, IT'S A *WHOPPER!*

FORGET IT, FRIEND! WHERE *ELSE* COULD I GET A WORKOUT LIKE THAT!

WORKOUT? WE ALL *NEEDED* THIS WORKOUT LIKE *THOR* NEEDS A *WIG!*

HE'S HALFWAY ACROSS TOWN BY NOW!

HE SAID SOMETHIN' ABOUT HAVIN' TO FIGHT SOME CREEP CALLED THE *WRECKER!**

--*SHEESH!*-- IT MUST TAKE A LOTTA *GUTS* TO WALK AROUND TOWN IN A *GET-UP* LIKE *THAT!*

AND, SPEAKING OF THAT ASGARDIAN HIPPIE--

WHERE IS HE?

*AND FIGHT HIM HE DOES, IN *THOR* #150,--SNEAK-A-PLUG STAN.

BUT WHAT ABOUT *DOOM?*

NOW THAT WE KNOW HE'S STILL *ALIVE,* WHY DON'T WE HIGHTAIL IT *AFTER* 'IM?

WE CAN'T INVADE THE SOVEREIGNTY OF HIS OWN *NATION,* BEN!

--*HUNH!*-- LOOKS TO *ME* LIKE YA WOULDN'T IF YA *COULD*-- LEASTWAYS NOT *NOW!*

AS LONG AS DOOM REMAINS IN *LATVERIA,* WE CAN'T *TOUCH* HIM!

AND, IF YOU FIND THIS ENDING TOO *MUSHY,* BELIEVER-- REMEMBER, OUR COSTUMED CAVORTERS ARE *MEN* FIRST, AND SUPERHEROES *SECOND!*--IN FACT... AREN'T WE *ALL?*

MMMM... I HOPE HE STAYS THERE *FOREVER!*

...AND WITH THAT FINAL THOUGHT WE MUST ONCE AGAIN BID FAREWELL TO THE COSMIC POWERED QUARTET -- BUT NEVER FEAR, A NEW *FANTASTIC FOUR* POCKETBOOK WILL BE COMING SOON!

20

THE HISTORY OF MARVEL
IN YOUR HANDS!